Billion-Dollar Matches

The one thing money can't buy? Love!

Finding true love is *never* easy. But when you're famous, it's even harder... So, M is here to help! M is a dating agency with a twist. They offer, to the rich and famous, a chance to date away from the limelight. And it's this promise of absolute discretion that compels *every* A-lister to keep them on speed dial.

M's founder, Madison Morgan, is no stranger to the red carpet herself. A former child actress, Madison knows—better than anyone!—the value of privacy. Which makes her an expert at finding the *most* idyllic and secluded locations for her clients. From Lake Geneva to the Seychelles, and Puerto Rico to Indonesia, Madison creates the perfect backdrop to a couple's love story. And, just maybe, her own?

Fall in love with...

The Princess and the Rebel Billionaire
by Sophie Pembroke

Surprise Reunion with His Cinderella
by Rachael Stewart

Caribbean Nights with the Tycoon
by Andrea Bolter

Available now!

Indonesian Date with the Single Dad
by Jessica Gilmore

Coming soon!

Dear Reader,

It has been my pleasure and delight to work with three other authors to bring you this fun miniseries, Billion-Dollar Matches, about the M dating agency, matchmakers to the world's elite. The agency's founder, Madison Morgan, plays a part in each of the books. In mine, without providing even a photograph of the other person or knowledge of where they're headed, Madison sends Charlie Matthews and Luna Price to the exotic Caribbean island of Puerto Rico.

Convinced they desire nothing more than a casual week of rest and relaxation, neither intends for real feelings to emerge—they both have horrors and secrets they need to move past. But among the fun in the sun, scrumptious food, historical sights and magical midnights, their barriers begin to slip away. And after the week that changes their lives, they test their feet in new waters at Luna's home in Los Angeles. But nothing goes according to plan for these two and it takes several rounds of their trying to get it right. Do you think that they will?

As always, thanks for reading!

Andrea x

Caribbean Nights
with the Tycoon

—

Andrea Bolter

Special thanks and acknowledgment are given to
Andrea Bolter for her contribution to the
Billion-Dollar Matches miniseries.

HARLEQUIN®

Romance™

Recycling programs
for this product may
not exist in your area.

ISBN-13: 978-1-335-40675-0

Caribbean Nights with the Tycoon

Copyright © 2021 by Harlequin Books S.A.

This edition published by arrangement with Harlequin Books S.A.

For questions and comments about the quality of this book,
please contact us at CustomerService@Harlequin.com.

Harlequin Enterprises ULC
22 Adelaide St. West, 40th Floor
Toronto, Ontario M5H 4E3, Canada
www.Harlequin.com

Printed in U.S.A.

Andrea Bolter has always been fascinated by matters of the heart. In fact, she's the one her girlfriends turn to for advice with their love lives. A city mouse, she lives in Los Angeles with her husband and daughter. She loves travel, rock 'n' roll, sitting at cafés and watching romantic comedies she's already seen a hundred times. Say hi at andreabolter.com.

Books by Andrea Bolter

Harlequin Romance

Visit the Author Profile page at Harlequin.com.

For Ramona

CHAPTER ONE

"*BIENVENIDO*, SENORITA. WELCOME to Recurso Llave Dorada—the Golden Key Resort."

The mustached man in a yellow blazer offered Luna Price his greeting as soon as she stepped out of the limo. As she did, her eyes quickly darted left and right so she could be sure she wasn't being observed. Force of habit. Even though she was here through an arrangement with the exclusive M Dating Agency, all of whose clients were apparently rich and famous, Luna wanted to be certain that she wouldn't be recognized.

Without meticulously done hair, makeup and styling, she hoped she looked like a typical tourist. The hat, dark glasses, simple sundress and sandals she wore should serve as help. Even though she'd been out of the media's eye for quite a while, she'd never forget the unforgiving judgment the press gave a film star's appearance.

"I am Juan Carlos Ortiz, Dorada's manager," the gentleman Luna stood opposite continued. Embroidered above his jacket's pocket was the resort's logo of two palm trees, one leaning left and the other right, with a gold key across them. "Kindly follow me to a private reception area reserved exclusively for our M guests."

That was a good start in ensuring Luna's privacy. "Gracias."

While guests milled about in the area through the wide-open wooden doors, which allowed the check-in area to feel like an extension of the outdoors, Juan Carlos gestured for Luna to follow him to the right. "I trust everything about your journey to us was satisfactory?"

"It was." Indeed, Madison Morgan and her M Dating Agency had thought of every detail to make Luna's trip pleasant, despite her own apprehensions. A discreet SUV had picked her up from her parents' ranch outside of Louisville, Kentucky, as a limo would have drawn too much attention, and the chartered airplane that departed from a private terminal had every imaginable comfort.

As was Madison's design, Luna was to spend a secluded week with a man she'd never met and knew nothing about. And she hadn't been told until the plane was soaring through the air that she'd be doing it in the archipelago of Caribbean islands known as Puerto Rico. This was how M did business, arranging ultraprivate rendezvous for the elite around the globe. Although the entire prospect made Luna uneasy, the exotic destination had her interest piqued.

"This way, please." Juan Carlos held open a door on the side of the building and Luna stepped through. It was a salon-type room with two wooden desks beveled with designs of pineapples, a symbol of hospitality, and plush armchairs with yellow upholstered cushions. Large paintings of native flora and fauna decorated the walls. Open windows gave the space a light feel. She quickly observed that, with one exception, the few other people in this private reception area all wore yellow blazers, identifying them as resort staff. Juan Carlos gestured to a desk, then pulled out a chair and invited Luna to sit, which she would have done had she not been stopped dead in her tracks. Because when she caught sight of the tall man across the room wearing a business shirt and trousers—the one person not wearing the yellow blazer—she was unable to move.

It wasn't just that he was good-looking, which he certainly was—in Luna's line of work, attractiveness was an everyday commodity, and she'd learned the hard way that it had nothing to do with a person's character. There was something different about this man, though—he had a stature and commanding presence that had little to do with his physical gifts. It was as if the entire room was centered around him, as the employees fumbled over themselves to take the small travel bag he held, an offer he refused. "Thank you, no," he said in a low baritone. Another tried to hand him a drink, but he shook his head in rejection. "Thank you, no," he repeated, with a bit of impatience in his voice now.

Juan Carlos presented Luna with a large bouquet of tropical flowers. "Once again, welcome."

As she brought them to her nose to appreciate their fragrance, the tall man who was garnering all of the attention glanced to her. While she'd already noticed his close-cropped thick brown hair and long-limbed muscular build, once he focused his emerald-green eyes on her, something tugged at her heart. "Gracias for the flowers," she whispered.

Instantly, she hoped against that he was not the man she'd been matched up with for the week. No, he was too innately impressive, too statuesque. The last thing Luna wanted was to feel pressure to be perfect for a powerful man, one with expectations and specifications. It was that very thing she needed to stay away from. She was not here to please someone, nor was she open to wanting to.

But two things occurred to her as the man's pointed stare became impossible to deny and their eyes met. One was the unconfirmed yet somehow undeniable knowledge that they were, in fact, each other's match for the week. The second was that while his exquisite face did rival that of a Greek god's, there was pain behind his eyes and in the set of his jaw. There was much simmering under his surface.

Juan Carlos, sensing the scrutiny his two guests were bestowing on each other, said,

"We generally introduce M's guests to each other once they've reached their villa but you two seem to have met." *Met* wasn't exactly the right word. Luna had consented to M's conditions that she would not so much as see a photo or hear the name of the person with whom she'd be spending the week until they arrived at their destination. She trusted Madison's ability to unite people who were not only compatible, but also shared the same goals for the match. Which meant that he wasn't here to meet the love of his life, either. That was good. Luna had made it clear to Madison that she was seeking a week of easygoing companionship and that was it.

"Yes, we have." The words fell trancelike from the green-eyed man's mouth. He removed himself from the staff huddle and stepped toward Luna, where he presented his outstretched palm for a handshake. "Charlie."

"Luna." Managing the enormous bouquet with one hand, she joined her other with his. The contact with his large, thick-skinned hand gave off more sparks than she wished. Not finding him appealing at all would have been ideal. The seven days were supposed to be a safe getaway for Luna. A segue back into casual dating. An escape where she could just be herself, not worry about her image or her appearance or anything other than short-term relaxation and enjoyment.

So she had hoped that she wouldn't even find her match attractive or intriguing. That would have been the easiest way to proceed. Now, faced with the reality of a magnetic man with hurt in his eyes standing before her, Luna had the impulse to run back to the limo and immediately return to the hidden safety of her parents' ranch, where she'd been for the better part of a year. She knew that she couldn't, though, that it was time to move forward. And, what's more, she was ready to do so. But now, with this man in front of her, she had the instant suspicion that the next week was going to be different than what she'd bargained for unless she kept her guard up.

"Senor and senorita, if you'll come with me, a golf cart will take you to your villa. The luggage has already been delivered." Luna looked to Juan Carlos, almost silently pleading for him to get her out of this situation. As many strangers as Luna had to meet in her line of work, this would be far more personal. And, therefore, terrifying. Their villa? Had she been crazy in letting Anush, her best friend and personal stylist, talk her into this agreement? It suddenly seemed so.

As they moved toward the waiting golf cart, Charlie absentmindedly placed his hand on her upper arm to guide her out of the salon. She bristled. It had been a long time since a man had touched her beyond a handshake, and it was still something she wasn't comfortable with. It hadn't even occurred to her that this week might put that to the test, as well—whether or not she was ready for physical contact with a man. In any case, the feel of his fingertips was both scary and thrilling, and wholly unwelcome. She moved away.

Juan Carlos made sure his guests were situated in the back seat of the cart before he took his place in the front beside the driver, and then off they went.

"Where did you fly in from?" Luna fumbled to make small talk. She hoped she hadn't offended him by rejecting his guiding hand, but she'd be establishing as many boundaries as she needed to.

"Heathrow. I live in Buckinghamshire," he answered with a polite chill in his voice that didn't match the warm skin she could feel sitting next to her. "A little over an hour's drive from London." It was only then that Luna clearly heard his British accent. Madison and the M Dating Agency's policy was that participants had to put their complete faith in her abilities, as they'd learn nothing about their matches ahead of time. So all she now knew was that Charlie was English, had big hands and a second golf cart's worth of emotional baggage. He was obviously wealthy or he wouldn't have been able to afford Madison's hefty fee. What more would she be discovering about him, and when?

"Yourself?" he asked as if it required effort.

"Kentucky," she answered without going into the details. It was her childhood home and the place where she'd spent the past twelve months.

"American. Have we met before?" He studied her. "You look familiar."

"Senor and senorita, may I present La Villa de Felicidad?"

"Wonderful," Luna murmured.

* * *

Juan Carlos gestured with a grand sweep of his hand once the golf cart came to a stop in front of the secluded structure at the end of the resort's property. Through a gate and far removed from any other buildings was its own sparkling cove, and no doubt a private beach. Charlie hadn't lost the headache that had joined him on his flight, although he couldn't fail to notice the spectacular setting where he was to spend the coming week.

The sky was a soft blue under which the gentle waves of the Caribbean glistened in the sunshine. "Oh, my…" Luna let the comment slip as they exited the golf cart, and Charlie had to agree. He'd been told accommodations would be at one of the Golden Key Concierges' luxury properties but hadn't known exactly what to expect. They followed Juan Carlos into the villa—*into* being a relative term as the enormous living space was completely open, with fresh air flowing through a secluded courtyard on one side and the beachfront on the other.

"Where are the walls?" Luna asked.

Juan Carlos quickly showed them to a wood cupboard near the entrance that contained an elaborate control panel and electronic devices. "Each wall, as well as portions of the ceiling, are fully retractable. They also provide shading options and climate control for the hotter parts of the day. Please utilize these choices however you wish. May I give you a demonstration?"

"Thank you, but I think I can figure it out." Charlie Matthews, CEO of his own biotech empire, AMgen, one of the largest in the UK and Europe, ought to be able to figure out how to retract a ceiling.

"*Bueno.* Would you like a tour of the villa or would you prefer to explore it yourself?"

"Let's have a quick look."

"The lounging and dining area." Juan Carlos pointed from right to left. "If it's acceptable, your personal chef and butlers will introduce themselves a bit later to obtain your preferences."

"Fine."

"Shall I assume you'd prefer dinner here in your villa rather than at one of our restaurants on the property?"

"Yes," Luna said quickly.

Juan Carlos led them farther inside. "And may I present the master bedroom."

"There's only one bed," Luna blurted out.

"Yes." Charlie looked around, estimating

the villa's layout, and dreaded to ask, as he hoped the resort manager would intuit the situation. "Where are the other bedrooms?"

"Only this sumptuous master suite, senor. The villa was chosen specifically for you by Ms. Morgan."

"It won't do for us," Luna interjected.

"I'm sorry, senorita. Ms. Morgan has made all of the arrangements. Perhaps you'd like to speak with her."

"We will," Charlie replied shortly.

"Either way, I regret to inform you that none of the resort's other accommodations are even close in regard to the luxury and privacy of this villa and, in any case, we have no vacancies whatsoever."

So, Madison had kept this trick up her sleeve. Even though he, and presumably Luna, had clarified that they were not interested in using this week for a romantic tryst, the matchmaker had her own ideas.

"Wonderful," he quipped sarcastically.

The journey, the ride from the airport, the overeager staff and now the prospect of a week with a stranger and one bed was all crashing down on him. He was ready for Juan Carlos to take his leave. There was to be no tipping or money exchanged during this weeklong getaway, as all costs and gratuities had been taken care of previously, so their business was done.

"I'll bid you adios, then. I am at your disposal for anything you need. The golf cart will be left for your use and you'll find a video with Ms. Morgan's suggested activities for your stay. I hope you'll find the accommodations spacious enough to meet your needs and that your week with us at Dorada exceeds your expectations."

Much as he wanted him to depart, as soon as the manager left, Charlie's stomach lurched. This was really happening. It had been his right-hand man, and AMgen's COO, Tom Khatri, who had suggested that Charlie undertake this M Dating Agency excursion. But now that he was here, he wasn't sure how he'd get through it. A week with a woman he didn't even know? And why did she look so familiar? He was sure he'd met her before. The awkwardness of being alone with her was already uncomfortable.

Luna was still wearing her hat and sunglasses but he could see she was a willowy beauty, tall and very slim. Her floral cotton dress was hardly what he'd have expected a client of M's to be wearing, as the agency catered to a population that likely shopped at the world's most select boutiques. After they stood facing each other in a silence that became excruciating, he finally asked, "Did I notice that you speak Spanish?"

"Enough to get by, *más o menos*."

"When did you learn?"

"I studied it in school. Living in Los Angeles, where there are a lot of different languages spoken, gives me a chance to stay in practice."

"Los Angeles? Didn't you say you arrived here from Kentucky?" That seemed a bit suspect to him. He'd been to the States enough times to know that Kentucky was quite different from California.

"I, uh… My permanent home is Los Angeles. I've spent some prolonged time in Kentucky that's now come to an end." If that had been an attempt to clear up the confusion, her tone suggested the opposite.

She removed her hat and sunglasses, allowing him to see her in full for the first time. Sun-kissed blond locks cascaded past her shoulders in waves, framing her face. And such a pretty face it was, with big blue eyes, flawless skin and perfectly bowed lips. It looked as if she was without makeup, another thing that surprised him given M's reputation for attracting the polished crème de la crème from every corner of the globe. Charlie actually quite liked that she appeared so natural. It reminded him of a casual comfort he used to know, and something he missed so much the tears he thought had finally dried up threatened to reappear.

Now that he saw Luna's full face and hair, the sense that he knew her nagged at him again.

He realized he was staring when she broke in and asked, "Do you speak any Spanish yourself?"

"To order in a restaurant, maybe. I suppose I'll need your assistance this week."

"I'll do my best." She licked her lips in what seemed like a nervous response. It was quite inappropriate that he found the move sensual, but he wished she would do it again.

He looked out to the blue water and clean sand, which was visible from throughout the villa. "Well, these surroundings could hardly be lovelier."

"Yes. I don't know anything about Puerto Rico."

"It's interesting that Madison doesn't tell the participants where their destination will be."

"Yes, my friend and stylist, Anush, made all the arrangements. She knew about the agency." Ah, she had a stylist. That sounded more like M's clientele. Although she made a point of calling her a friend, too. That didn't seem like the behavior of any of the upper crust he'd ever known.

"Similarly, my COO, Tom, handled the details on my end." Blather seemed the only option. He was so out of practice in spending social time with a woman—with anyone really—that he didn't know what to talk about. And she wasn't helping any, giving short answers as her eyes glanced all around the villa. She wasn't going to make this easy on him. He wondered what criteria Madison used for her matchmaking. Did she look for people who were opposite types from each other, or ones that were more alike? Because something beyond the comely features of Luna's face told him that she might have as many demons to battle as he did. "Let me try to reach Madison and sort out this lodging situation."

"Yes, thank you."

He pulled his phone from his pocket but the call went to voice mail so he left a message and then sent a text. "We'll have to wait for someone to get back to us." He opened his carry-on bag and took out his laptop.

"What sort of business are you in?"

"I have a biotech company."

"Would I have heard of it?"

"AMgen. We're mainly in the UK and Europe."

"AMgen. Well, of course, I've heard of it. Hasn't everyone? Charlie. Right. I think I read an article about you in a magazine. Charlie Matthews."

"Yes."

A magazine. Was that where he'd seen a photo of her, as well? Madison had mentioned that public figures needing the utmost discretion often used her service. Luna? Luna? It hit him like a ton of bricks. "Luna! Of course. You're Luna Price! I've seen some of your movies."

Juan Carlos must have taken the tropical breeze with him when he left because the air had gone still. Luna knew she was imagining it, as she could see the glorious palm trees swaying outside of the villa. It was just the finality that she, Charlie, this resort and Puerto Rico were going to be a unit for the next week. And now he'd recognized her. It was one thing to agree to this adventure in theory and quite another to be standing in the middle of it.

"While I understand that Madison works with a very select clientele, I somehow wasn't expecting a movie star." He said it as if he was aggravated.

"Sorry to disappoint." She shrugged snidely.

Now that he'd placed her, here it came. Once people knew she was Luna Price, film actress, everything seemed to change. They gushed all over her and stumbled over their words, and started treating her as if she was some kind of otherworldly creature who didn't bleed red or have the same ten fingers and ten toes they did. While, at the same time, they examined her as if she was a product that they had to decide if it was worth spending their money on or not. Luna was, of course, grateful for the life of privilege her fame had brought her, but deep inside it never got easier to be constantly measured and judged.

"I didn't mean it like that," Charlie retorted. "I'm just a bit shocked."

Although she'd been on dozens of film sets, where she'd had to meet cast and crew members for the first time, and had interacted with hundreds of fans, the ineptness she was feeling now was somehow different. Maybe because Charlie Matthews appeared to have a distant and absolute power. Since people usually fumbled all over her, the dynamic wasn't something she was used to.

"So we've established it then," she spat out. "I'm an actress and you're a tech genius."

"Genius. Yes." He snickered.

"And here we are." Ugh, Luna couldn't think of a time when she'd felt more off-kilter. She and tall, handsome, prickly Charlie Matthews were to spend seven nights alone together? She'd just like to get through the next five minutes. "I assume that Madison explained to you that I'm not using her services to find a long-term romantic match."

"Neither am I." She couldn't snap that out fast enough.

"I'm only seeking a sort of transitional week of rejuvenation."

"Exactly. Transitional." How were they going to begin that promised relaxation? Luna's shoulders felt as tense as coils.

"Which is why it doesn't make sense that she booked us a place with only one bed."

"No insult intended but I'm not comfortable with that."

"I understand completely."

His eyes met hers but then ricocheted around the lounging area of the villa, as if he was trying to fix on something other than her.

She decided to break the stalemate. "I've never been to the Caribbean. Have you?"

"No. Do you travel a lot for your films?"

"A fair amount shoot right in LA. Others in Canada. And then for a few others I've gone on location."

"That must be exciting."

"It has its moments. I've been very lucky."

She wasn't ready to tell him yet that the first movie she was going to shoot after a year off was starting up right after this week in Puerto Rico. Or why that was so. Although she had a strange sensation that she and Charlie might get to know each other this week more than she had anticipated. There was something about him she couldn't put her finger on that made her feel she might want to genuinely talk to him, and listen. He had a sort of seriousness that she liked. She might need to keep reminding herself that this was no time to get caught up in someone. She was taking care of herself now and was nowhere near being willing to trust someone—she might never be. But each time his eyes shot away, her desire increased to have them back. There was a lot of story behind his green orbs—of that much she was certain.

"What sort of travel do you typically do?" she asked, continuing to chat, her breath easing. "Oh, and shall we have a cold drink?"

Juan Carlos had mentioned that the villa was fully stocked. They stepped over to a bar area that was done in rich woods with a bamboo ceiling fan overhead. Both of them were careful not to move too near to each other. Atop the marble counter were clear cylinders filled with juices that had slices of fresh fruit floating in them. Behind the bar was a coffee setup, with beans and teas from around the world. There was a wide array of rums. Luna recalled once reading that Puerto Rico was famous for its rum production. There were other spirits and liquors, too, from tequila to gin to aged scotch. All sorts of sodas and mixers were visible through the bar refrigerator's glass doors as were at least a half-dozen bottles of top-of-the-line champagne, along with a visible compartment that displayed gallons of ice cubes ready to help chill the hot August day.

Luna knew that she was nervous and, as such, took such a scrupulous inventory of the beverages. She resisted moving on to the open kitchen area, where gourmet and local food and snacks were bound to be overflowing. Being around a lot of food was potentially challenging for her, so she'd have to be diligent about the techniques she used to keep from reverting to old behaviors. She squelched the bubbling feeling in her stomach that served as a warning sign.

"Those juices look inviting," Charlie decided after glancing over the options.

"Yes, one is guava and the other is orangelo, a combination of orange and pomelo," Luna informed him as she read the scripted cards placed in front of each canister.

"Pomelo is similar to grapefruit. That sounds like a refreshing blend. Would you like some over ice?" He took the lead and selected two tall glasses that had the resort's logo etched on them.

"Gracias."

The corner of his mouth ticked up. When he had said he'd need her assistance this week because she spoke a bit of Spanish, a squiggle had crept up her spine. She'd been able to keep any expression from registering in her face, being an actress and all. But the idea of Charlie obliged to her in any way shocked her with possibility. Made her think of people who relied on each other, who finished each other. Who had the kind of real-life connection that Luna only knew how to act out in front of a camera.

Charlie Matthews was probably not beholden to anything or anyone. Luna noted to herself that she'd better not allow even a moment of fantasizing that this weeklong dip into the waters of dating was anything else. It already seemed that was going to be harder than it sounded with Charlie. His stoic posture, with that straight torso, was already making her think about being in his embrace. Her head against his no-doubt taut and solid chest. She even imagined what her lips might feel like against his. She was sure his would be firm yet alive. Shaking her head a bit, she snapped out of that thinking, almost ready to laugh at her own imagination. Wow, she hadn't been alone with a man in a long time.

"The chef is coming by to serve dinner at eight?" he asked, already knowing the answer because it was written on an information note left on the bar. "It's after five now. Shall we enjoy the juice while we familiarize ourselves with the villa and then perhaps have a rest? It's been a long day of travel."

Bartender Charlie moved behind the bar and filled each glass halfway with ice, then poured the orangelo drink. It was already delicious, and she hadn't even tasted it. The juice didn't look half-bad, either.

She moved closer to him, although with the bar between them, it was as if he was the server and she the customer. But when he handed her the drink and their fingers brushed, the playacting ended there. It brought her body to attention. The touch of Charlie's fingers as he handed her the ice-cold drink felt like a key to a door that she didn't know was locked.

CHAPTER TWO

JUICE IN HAND, Charlie gestured for Luna to follow him so that they could further explore the villa's features. He'd mentioned taking a rest afterward and as soon as he'd said it, the vibrations around them changed, as if they both realized the implications of sharing this space. Charlie hadn't spent time anywhere with anyone in a long while and had spooked even himself with the thought of them *resting* together under the same roof. As they strolled from the airy and opulent living and dining areas toward the gigantic master bedroom, the realization that the sleeping arrangements were still unresolved pounded between his ears.

"That has to be the biggest bed I've ever seen," Luna quipped. She followed with a quick sip of her drink, which she gripped tightly with both hands as if it was a security blanket. With the walls retracted in the bed-room and the warm wind flowing through, locks of her hair floated a little bit this way and that way. Charlie was sure they would be like spun silk to the touch. Low in his belly, a charge ignited, one that had been dormant for as long as he could remember. No, that wasn't true. He remembered exactly when that part of him had turned to ash.

The bed had four wooden posts and was made up with colorful bedding, some in a bright red floral fabric and others in a muted green-leaf design. Two low armchairs flanked a round table—it served as a sitting area and was positioned to view the private courtyard secluded by tall hedges. In the center of the courtyard, a table and chairs sat next to a Spanish fountain. Off to the side was a sparkling swimming pool, with everything fully enclosed for use by only the two of them. Charlie had stayed in deluxe accommodations all over the world but this had to be the most lavish.

"You'll sleep in here, of course." Given Juan Carlos's report that there were no other vacancies on the property, he felt the need to reassure Luna. "If we don't change to another setup."

"A romantic hideaway all to myself. How ironic."

"You might enjoy the amenities." This was no easier on him than it was on her.

"Yes, I will. Thank you. I just meant… I don't know what I meant." Her lips, glistening from the juice, took another sip. "Since Madison knew we weren't interested in being…physical, it's interesting that she chose this for us."

"I counted six overstuffed sofas throughout that immense living-room area. I'm sure any one of them will make a comfortable bed."

"So…you plan to sleep in the living room?"

"If need be. Surely we're not going to sleep in the same bed." That came out harsher than he'd intended. Luna's head leaned back, as if she was dodging the words. Ironic romantic getaway, indeed. He was busy telling one of the world's most beautiful actresses that, under no circumstances, was he going to lie down beside her.

They moved on to the expertly appointed master bathroom and then the kitchen, with its top-of-the-line appliances. After inspecting everything, Luna said, "Juan Carlos explained when I arrived that we'll have a personal chef bring our meals or prepare them here."

"Yes, that's why I had suggested that we both rest a bit and then dress for dinner. Although since we're eating alone, should it be casual attire?" Charlie was again reminded that he didn't know how to act around a woman in an informal setting, and the impending dinner was feeling like a challenge. He was so out of practice communicating with someone unless it was about work. In fact, there'd only ever been one woman he'd cared to behave properly around, and with her everything had been natural and easy. He was the boss to a large staff of employees, but knew how to keep himself at a distance. His entire inventory of social manners needed an overhaul.

"Casual sounds great," Luna replied.

A couple of hours later, Charlie sat up from where he was lying on the sofa when he heard a voice at the villa's entrance. "Senor, it's Chef Diego here, may I come in?" Charlie rubbed his face with his open palms. He hadn't been woken up by the chef's call, because Charlie didn't sleep...ever. But he'd surprised himself. With the mild afternoon and the sound of waves ebbing and flowing at the shore, he'd achieved a meditation that had transported him out of consciousness. As he stood, he began to tuck his shirt back into his trousers, but then, on impulse, decided not to.

"Yes, Chef. Come in."

Diego wheeled a cart into the villa, and was followed by another staffer with a second cart who left after his delivery.

Luna strode out of the bedroom. She must have heard that their visitor had arrived. "Ah, you're ahead of me," Charlie said, pointing to her change of clothes.

"The rainforest shower is just marvelous." Charlie would follow suit after the meeting with the chef and absolutely refused to imagine Luna naked in the shower in the meantime.

"You look beautiful." He hadn't really meant to do more than think that sentiment, but he hadn't been able to censor himself in time.

Luna was a sight for sore eyes. She wore a long, straight midnight blue dress, as simple as could be. It fell like a column down her tall narrow body. She looked even more stunning than she had earlier in her sundress earlier. She was very slim, with neither womanly hips or large breasts. With those shiny blond waves loose around her enchanting face, and barefoot, she was the picture of unaffected beauty. It was still hard to reckon that she was a glamorous movie star who wore designer gowns to awards shows and diamonds from the world's most famous jewelers. Here, in this private retreat, she was unrecognizable. Which was apparently how she wanted it.

"I didn't know how to pack for this trip to an unknown destination. So I brought a little of everything."

"Senor and senorita, it will be my pleasure to be your dining manager while you are with us at Dorada. It was indicated on your reservation that both of you are interested in sampling the flavors of Puerto Rico. Is that correct?"

They both nodded. Charlie felt like he'd been eating the same five dishes his housekeeper prepared for him for years now, with him not caring enough to speak to her about expanding her repertoire. Food had been simple fuel—one thing tasted the same as the next. When Tom convinced him to fly off to an unknown destination under the M

Dating Agency's direction, the promise of unusual food had piqued his interest. He was glad that Luna had confirmed herself as game, too.

"I've brought some samplings I hope are to your liking. May I start you off with Puerto Rico's signature cocktail, the piña colada?"

Charlie had tasted that drink, rich with coconut milk and pineapple juice, before. While delicious, he thought it too sweet and heavy for dinner.

"Diego, perhaps tomorrow. Can you suggest a wine for tonight?"

"Of course, senor. I brought a couple of bottles."

"I'm so hungry," Luna chimed in. "I can't even talk about food without eating some. Do you have any snacks we can munch on?"

"Camarones al ajillo." Diego removed a tray that was being kept warm on a burner from his cart. Luna wasted no time in grabbing one of the succulent shrimp with her fingers and biting in.

"Que sabor," she said, signaling her approval. "The garlic. And goodness, I needed some protein."

"With our heritage deriving from Spanish, indigenous Taino and the African peoples, we have a rich culinary tradition," Diego explained. "If I may serve it, I've made for you tonight one of Puerto Rico's most beloved preparations, *arroz con gandules*, a dish of rice, pigeon peas and a *sofrito* of peppers, onions, aromatics and herbs. Along with a slow-roasted *pernil*—marinated pork shoulder. And for dessert, coconut pudding."

"Sounds great," she said.

"Might I suggest this pinot noir?" The chef presented a bottle. Charlie read the label and nodded.

Diego went about setting up the dining table in the courtyard, which was now bathed in the glow of moonlight. Charlie's phone rang. "It's Madison," he told Luna and stepped inside, away from the chef, wanting to keep the conversation private.

"Yes, we arrived safely. But we are dissatisfied with the sleeping arrangements. Luna assures me she made the same thing clear to you, as I did—that we are not her for a romantic liaison."

"Charlie, I always book my couples into a master suite. Anything can happen," Madison replied.

"Nothing is going to happen."

"Didn't you agree to leave things up to me?"

"Yes, but I would prefer not to be manipulated."

"I'm sure you'll find a way to be contented."

He supposed he could insist she find another resort. But the sofa would really suit him fine. "All right, Madison."

"Just relax, Charlie. Have an open mind. Give in to the island."

He returned, frustrated, to Luna and reported what Madison had said.

"I'm going to take a shower. I'll claim the other bathroom off the kitchen. I'll meet you at the fountain at eight?"

"Sounds charming," she giggled with an innocent blush.

"It wasn't supposed to be."

After the words fell from his mouth, he wished he could have taken them back.

"The candles and the moonlight provide perfect lighting," Luna said as she and Charlie sat at the wrought-iron table and chairs beside the courtyard fountain.

"Says the cinema professional."

She snickered a little. Charlie hadn't figured out Luna Price yet. She was nothing like he'd expect from a movie star. As she fidgeted with the voluminous shawl she'd thrown over her sleeveless blue dress, she seemed almost awkward. Not the confident beauty she projected onscreen. Illusion, he figured. Smoke and mirrors. He hadn't seen many of her movies so he wouldn't assume to know her public persona, let alone her private one. Which wasn't to say that her attractiveness was anything but undeniable. In fact, under the moon she was almost unbearably lovely.

"The *arroz con gandules* is delicious," she said.

"I'd never heard of pigeon peas before, so when Chef Diego explained the recipe, I was apprehensive."

"I thought I'd heard of a famous old-timey dish called pigeon under glass but then I remembered it was pheasant under glass."

He chuckled. "Neither sounds very appetizing."

"No. They don't." She turned her attention back to her food and took several bites, which she chewed slowly and with determination. "Pigeon peas are not that different to green peas. I like the peppers and herbs in this dish."

"Very flavorful."

Her shawl slipped down one arm again, revealing a velvety shoulder that looked even nicer in the flickering of the candles . She quickly righted the covering, though in a self-conscious way, as if she'd accidentally revealed a part of her body she didn't want seen. Rather strange for someone whose likeness was displayed on megascreens throughout the world.

After his shower, Charlie had slipped into khakis and a new white T-shirt, one of the many items his housekeeper had bought when he'd sent her to buy him a tourist's wardrobe, unsure what he'd need. He felt odd in his bare feet on the stone courtyard tiles, having taken Luna's cue in not putting on shoes. It seemed almost intimate, something only people who lived together did. Like he used to do. He wasn't the newfangled sort of tech billionaire who reported to his office in a hoodie and jeans. It was a suit and tie for him every day he went into town, which he did as infrequently as possible. He knew his formality was likely off-putting but it helped him keep his reserve, keep up the appearance of someone in control even though on the inside he was in tatters.

"I have to admit, I've only seen a few of your movies."

"Me, too."

"What do you mean?"

"I rarely watch my movies once I've shot them."

"Really? Why?"

"Because I'd only see flaws and things I wish I could do over again."

"I don't think anyone could accuse you of having flaws."

She giggled in that adorable way again. Luna had a kind of wholesomeness that continued to surprise him. "You have no idea how many of my imperfections the press and the worldwide web have documented well."

"Nonsense. They're all idiots."

Spearing some of the unctuous tender pork from his plate, he studied her some more. He hadn't had dinner alone with a woman in ages, in years. The figurative wounds that never healed reminded him of why. They made sure that if Charlie was enjoying himself or even just having a positive thought, the gashes would open again.

Reminding him of his loss. Recollecting the tragedy.

For the first time, Charlie wished the cuts could be at least bandaged over for a bit of respite. He knew that they would never disappear. But maybe it would be good for him if he didn't have to experience the radiating pain every moment of his life. He knew it was he himself who scratched at the sores, kept them from fading. That was his choice. It had become all he knew. The ache was so agonizing that it demanded his full attention, all day, every day. As a matter of fact, it's what had kept him inside his house for all these years. Night after night, just him and his anguish. There was almost a twisted comfort in it, because there was no risk. It was something he could count on. It was his vigil.

But tonight, looking at Luna's sexy shoulders as she continually fought with that shawl that didn't want her to be covered up, Charlie wondered if he could find a salve for his pain. Maybe Madison had a point. Maybe there was a chance that the warm embrace of Puerto Rico could ease him, even just a little.

"Tell me more about your flaws," Charlie

said, but the words had come out all wrong. What he wanted to ask was about how she handled being in the public eye. He knew needed to start interacting again with the outside world. Not long ago, Tom had insisted Charlie come into London for a face-to-face heart-to-heart, and had told him—as both COO and friend—that AMgen's investors were losing confidence in the sorrowful and reclusive CEO who scarcely left his estate. That they want a visible face for the business. That the company's messaging as innovators and limitless thinkers was losing credibility when the leader existed in seclusion. Some even directly said that he should be seen dating women. That idea was utterly overwhelming. Yet Charlie did understand that if he was going to keep his company strong he needed to move forward.

"Famous faces really are illusions," Luna said, breaking into his thoughts. "It might not be obvious to you but if you looked at a publicity photo of me next to how I look tonight, you might not think you were seeing the same person. When you hear it referred to as the glamour factory, that's no joke. It takes a whole crew to deliver Luna Price."

"Sounds exhausting."

Luna went completely silent. Charlie could have kicked himself. What a ridiculous thing to say to a woman who'd had so much success in her chosen profession. Tom was so right that Charlie was out of practice interacting. Perhaps it wasn't that he needed to become more social and at ease with people. It could be just the opposite. That he needed to relearn how to be a proper English gentleman. One who kept his thoughts to himself.

He hadn't put his communication skills to the test for a while. Maybe what had happened during those interminable nights alone in agony and loss was that he'd become someone incapable of bull. Someone who cut to the truth. It was his bluntness that had become disconcerting, not his aloofness.

Or maybe it was her. Luna. Even though he'd just met her, his subconscious had detected in her a link. That glaze in her eyes. Something was going on with her under the radar. She lived in Kentucky, yet she lived in Los Angeles. None of that made sense. Not that it was any of his business. "Luna, I'm sorry. I shouldn't have said that."

Her words came slowly and with an exhale. "Oh, no, you're right. It *is* horrible sometimes. The stress can be overwhelming. It's what led me to my..." She noticeably collected her thoughts and pulled up her shawl again. "My need to get away for a while."

This was supposed to be both easy and easygoing. Time to press the reset button. "Amen to that. After dinner, let's watch the video of suggested activities."

"After all," she said, "we're supposed to be here to have fun."

"Right. Fun." Charlie thought he might need to consult a dictionary. He couldn't remember the meaning of the word.

Once the last of the creamy coconut pudding had been consumed, Charlie and Luna regarded each other across the table. Conversation during the meal had been a combination of strange and fascinating. He'd asked some personal questions and she thought she'd done a good job of skirting what she didn't want to answer, a necessary skill she'd honed over the years. Although something inside her actually did want to communicate with him candidly, she hadn't really told him anything about her past or present. What witchery did Madison Morgan have up her sleeve? She seemed to have paired Luna with someone who sincerely touched her inside with every stare those dazzling green eyes bestowed.

"Would you like coffee?" Charlie asked, pointing to the thermos left by Diego, whose meal had left them wanting for nothing.

"No. Thanks." It was Luna's turn now to do the inquiring. Curiosity propelled her. "What motivated you to contact Madison's agency?"

"It was all my trusted COO, Tom, who has been with me since AMgen's beginnings."

"Just a buddy looking out for a buddy?"

Charlie blinked a couple of times. "I haven't done much dating in the last ten years. In fact, I haven't done any."

"Ten years. That's a long time. I'd think as a leader of a successful empire, you'd have women clamoring to make your acquaintance."

"Some opportunists have tried, I suppose."

"I know all about that."

"I'm sure you do."

"Ten years. Hmm. Is it too personal to ask, were you in a relationship before that?"

His jaw ticked. She could tell he was making a decision about how to answer. "I was married. At a very young age."

"Oh, I see. And things didn't work out."

"Not exactly." His eyes dropped to his empty dessert bowl.

She didn't know what, or what not, to say. "So after ten years, why now?" Luna pivoted away from more direct questions about Charlie's marriage, which he clearly didn't want to be interrogated about.

"Frankly, it's a business move. The reclusive —what was it you called me earlier— tech genius rattling around in his mansion isn't acceptable to our newer investors. And if we're going to continue to grow the company the way I promised, I need the expansion and shareholder support."

"What did you promise?"

Charlie's brow furrowed. "Do you always ask such probing questions?"

"Actually, no. I have to make superficial *nice-nice* with lots of people, all the time. And answer ridiculous yet personal questions."

"I'm intrigued. Such as what?"

"About the image. As I was telling you before, no one cares about the real me. They want to know about Luna Price. What is her day like? Does she wake up before dawn to exercise with her trainer? What does she eat? What kind of shampoo does she use? What famous actor or director will she be seen out on the town with?"

"I don't know how you handle the scrutiny."

"I don't. That is to say, I had to take a break from all of it. That's why I've been in Kentucky."

"Ah, so I've been hiding in Buckinghamshire and you in Kentucky."

"I was attending to some personal business."

"I see." He leaned back in his chair, professional enough not to probe further.

"Tech billionaire. Married young, divorced young. You're an interesting case."

"I didn't divorce."

"Sorry?"

Did that mean he was still married? Luna was sure Madison would have verified his marriage status. Did she work with clients who were still legally married but long separated from their spouses? It didn't much matter to Luna, as she was not looking toward anything further than this week, but she hated to think about other M clients being paired with someone who was still in an unresolved relationship. What did he mean by *hiding*?

He bit out, "Perhaps we've had enough getting to know each other for the evening. Let's watch the video."

And so, the two people who obviously had a lot of skeletons in their closets moved from the courtyard to inside the villa. A group of sofas and armchairs was arranged in a cluster for the best vantage point of the enormous wall-mounted TV.

Luna sat at the end of one sofa, her feet under her bent knees. Charlie hesitated but then sat at the other end of the same sofa. Using the remote control, he quickly found the channel they'd be using for their stay, which offered options such as dining and housekeeping. It was apparent that anything they required would be quickly proffered.

"*Bienvenido*. Welcome to the Recurso Llave Dorada," the narrator of the video greeted. And thus began a montage of the leisure pursuits and sights that Madison suggested they might enjoy during their visit.

"Madison asked me what types of activities I like participating in. Did she ask you the same?" Luna looked over to watch Charlie in profile as he kept his eyes on the screen. My, but he was attractive. His gravity was born of intelligence—that much she could tell. But that chiseled jaw almost worked to his disadvantage because it was distracting in its appeal. She bit her lip in embarrassment as she secretly pictured kissing her way across his perfect bone structure. That wasn't one of the activities on the menu.

"I enjoy culture and music." Charlie clicked on that option and the video showed people at an outdoor concert dancing to the Afro-Caribbean music Puerto Rico was famous for. Would she and Charlie dance together this week? Suddenly, she desperately wanted to. Next was a video traveling through the streets and past various historic monuments in the city of Old San Juan.

"I'm looking forward to visiting there."

"Yes. I see Madison gathered our preferences and chose destinations accordingly."

"I said I enjoy water."

He gestured outside, where the ever-present sound of the waves lapping onto the shore was a simple serenade. "Our own private beach."

And he clicked on the water-sports option for a montage of every conceivable form. One could sail, use Jet Skis, snorkel, scuba dive and paddleboard, just to name a few. A happy couple embraced and kissed under a waterfall. At that image, Charlie stood and sneered, "It's getting late. It looks like we'll have plenty to keep us occupied while we're here."

Clearly, he'd had enough of her company. She'd have her hands full this week, learning the cues from this unusual man. She stood and said, "Okay. I guess that's it then. I'll just go into the bedroom as we discussed."

"Yes, I'll be perfectly fine out here and there's the extra bathroom so I won't disturb you." Somehow, she was already disturbed. It felt a bit sad to be so brusquely banished to the bedroom. Rejected.

She headed toward that extravagant master suite, where she'd be sleeping alone. Was she secretly wishing this was, in fact, a romantic rendezvous to be spent with the perfect match with whom she would fall in love? If she was, she'd better get that idea out of her head right away, because that was definitely not on either of their itineraries. Still, as she moved it felt like a slow march toward emptiness. Her rational side told her it wouldn't feel that way once she got used to him. This was a beautiful paradise where she could breathe and just be with a man, and not worry about what he thought of her. She'd never see him again after this. That was the point. She needed to appreciate it as such. "Good night, Charlie," she said as she began to round the corner.

"Luna," he called before she was gone.

"Yes." She turned around to face him.

"I'm not divorced. I'm a widower. Ten years ago, my wife and baby daughter died."

The breath in her throat stilled. "Oh, my gosh. What an unimaginable tragedy." Her heart cracked for him. Before she knew it, she started to move back into the room.

But he dismissed her instantly. "Good night."

CHAPTER THREE

"THERE'S COFFEE," CHARLIE announced when Luna emerged from the bedroom in the morning. He was perched on a stool at the granite-topped island in the kitchen with his tablet open to company business. Luna's tan bare legs caught his eye. They were long and graceful, and she moved barefoot across the floor like a gazelle.

"What is this?" She pointed to a black thermos and stone mugs sitting on a wicker tray.

"Café *con leche* Dorada. That was the server's description when he delivered it."

"Have you been up long?"

Charlie would have laughed at that question if the answer wasn't so pathetic. Of course, he'd been up long—he'd barely slept a wink. Which was no reflection on the comfort of the sumptuous sofas or the villa's open walls that brought a pleasant coolness in the wee hours. No, it was that he hadn't slept in a decade, not really. Oh, he dozed and sleep did overtake his always ticking mind on occasion. But he never slumbered heavily, never woke feeling refreshed and certainly never experienced the optimistic sentiment that a new dawn had arrived. That was his lot—to be wide-awake. On guard. After his world changed forever on that snowy winter night so long ago.

"Yes. I called for breakfast and told the kitchen that unless we notified them further, they may choose our menus so that they include selections of traditional cuisine. I hope that's acceptable to you, otherwise we can certainly change it."

"No, that's great. My only request is that I eat at set meal times and have snacks available when I need them."

That struck Charlie as surprisingly rigid for an island holiday. He supposed that actresses both worried about their weight and were used to fitting in meals during film shoots. She was smart to have a routine. While Luna was very thin, he knew there was that old adage that the camera added weight. After she'd explained the glamour-factory standards she was held to, Charlie could hardly conceive of so many eyes on his appearance. Tom was the only one who had ever said anything to him about his, and that was just to suggest that Charlie dress down from the full suit and tie every time he went out. Which was why this morning he had chosen shorts and a loose linen shirt. He couldn't tell if the grey jersey T-shirt and shorts Luna wore were pajamas or morning loungewear. He did notice that she was not wearing a bra. A little twitch in his gut responded to that observation.

"There's fruit, eggs and *mallorca*, which are Puerto Rican sweet bread rolls. I can attest to their deliciousness."

She poured coffee and sipped from one of the mugs. "Oh, wow, I could get quite used to this."

Charlie's eyes widened. He knew Luna was only referring to the unusual coffee, which was rich, just a bit sweet and frothy with steamed milk. But somehow, her words brought a special meaning to his mind and got him thinking about what it might be like to *get quite used* to greeting someone in the morning. It might make sleepless nights more bearable, knowing there was someone to rise with once morning arrived.

"Would you like to snorkel today?" He was ready to make a plan. That would give him less time to mull over what his life wasn't. He was here with Luna to relax and recharge, and that was it. They might as well try to have a pleasant time.

"Sounds good," she answered in between bites from the plate she'd served herself.

Charlie had already downloaded the app that they'd use this week to his devices. With a couple of taps, he booked a boat to take them to a snorkeling spot. After changing into swimsuits and cover-ups, they slid into the golf cart and he drove them to the dock. A small private boat, preloaded with equipment plus some other provisions like towels, snacks and cold drinks on ice, awaited them. The captain helped Luna onto the deck of the pristine white boat, Charlie following right behind. They took seats on a comfortable bench covered in turquoise-colored leather.

The sky was bright and the water shimmering. Once the boat had reached a steady pace Luna looked pointedly into his eyes and asked, "Do you want to talk about it?"

"What's that?"

"Last night. When you said good-night. You told me about your wife and child. I didn't get a chance to fully express my sympathies."

He couldn't maintain eye contact so his gaze drifted to the waves that the boat cut through. His late wife, Amelia, would like this, to see that he was out on the open water, in the sunny air, rather than cooped up in his mansion with the curtains drawn, head burrowed in work under artificial lighting. He forced—indeed, forced—himself to glance back to Luna, whose eyes he could feel on him.

"Thank you."

"Does that have something to do with why you're a client of M?"

"According to my trusted team, I've grieved for too long. Apparently I've become lost in my hermit lifestyle, and our investors and stockholders are nervous about the future of the company."

"Is the future of the company what's important to you?"

"Why wouldn't it be?" he barked.

"Sorry," she said, recoiling. "I didn't mean anything by that. Only that you lost your family. Some people might let their business fall to the wayside after something like that."

"AMgen has always been a promise I made to my wife," he retorted.

"I'm being too nosy."

"Shall we just talk about the weather?" he chortled to himself. He knew that Tom was right—it was time for him to either resurrect himself or truly be put in a grave beside his long-gone wife and baby. "Ten years were more than enough to spend in mourning."

"I can't imagine how you've functioned after the accident. I think I'd fold up into myself."

"That's exactly what I've done. Yet somehow I grew the company from my cemetery of a mansion, where I concentrated on my work day and night, and nothing else. I told Amelia I'd see my vision through. It's only that vow to her that has kept me going."

"I'm sure she'd be very proud of you."

He cocked his head. Proud. Yes, she probably would be. He owed his accomplishments to her. She inspired him. When they'd married at nineteen, he promised he'd give her a life filled with security and joy. And, indeed, that's what they'd had. Until fate stole it away from them.

Was it actually possible for him to start relating to people more? Maybe build something, someday, with a new woman? Nothing serious, but someone to help him see light where there was only darkness. Last night, or maybe it had already been morning, long after he'd heard any sounds coming from the bedroom suite, he had been lying on the sofa, staring at the ceiling. And he'd thought about what he'd said to Luna and what she'd shared with him. About the pressure of the public eye. About the never-ending scrutiny. Of course, she had a blessed life to have reached that level of success, but he could tell she was fighting her own inner battles. That made Charlie feel less alone. For the first time in ten years. It was somehow both a comfort and a shock to be with her.

The boat stopped once it reached the coral reef that was a renowned snorkeling spot. "I'm excited," she said as the captain came on deck to fit them with the masks, snorkels and fins they'd need. Once suited up, they lowered themselves into the water. As they submerged to see what worlds thrived under the sea, Charlie acknowledged that he hadn't done anything like this in an eternity. Couldn't he allow a little bit of adventure back into his life?

Under the water with an English tech billionaire. Luna could hardly believe the dichotomies in her life. Here she was after a year spent at her parents' ranch in Kentucky, with her daily therapy and coaching appointments, and Anush staying there with her for moral support. Soon she'd be returning to her life in Los Angeles, where her fame and fortune rested on the box-office count of her next movie release or latest magazine cover. And at the moment she was submerged in the Caribbean with this somber widower, who was as troubled as she was.

The undersea life surrounding them was magical. Brightly colored fish swam in schools, sometimes just a few in a group, yet other times what looked like hundreds of babies. Turtles waded by the alive reefs. It was wonderful to ponder their existence, which was far different from the lives of humans. This was good for her soul, Luna concluded.

Every so often, she and Charlie would turn to each other as if to comment on what they were seeing. His swath of dark hair swooshed as he swam. She couldn't help admiring the way the angular muscles of his back flexed as he moved through the water. He reached to pull her toward a display of boldly hued parrotfish. Holding hands with him under the water and watching the awe-inspiring show in front of them was a poignant experience she wouldn't soon forget.

"That was fantastic," she exclaimed when they popped their heads above water and removed their equipment.

"Incredible." He nodded. With the captain's help they returned to the boat deck. As they dried themselves with towels, the captain put out a spread of cold water and snacks. Luna whisked on her cover-up. Charlie slung a towel low around his hips and remained shirtless, the water droplets glinting on his golden skin, reminding Luna that she hadn't been physical with a man in ages. The recovery program she'd been going through demanded that she focus only on herself. But the dearth had been easy because she could no longer stand the type of men she'd been dating. Men she was sure would have little interest in her if she hadn't been a celebrity. Troy Lutt being the latest of that ilk. Most everyone in Luna's life was around to try to capitalize on what association with her would bring. Troy had taken that to a new low.

She most definitively wasn't planning to bring a man into her life. Though it was impossible for her to divert her mind from imagining touching Charlie's smooth-looking skin, and running her hands down the physique she'd watched so deftly glide through the water. She bit back a giggle at her private little thoughts, so opposite to her declared intention for the week. It was a sneaky yet harmless bit of amusement, though.

Once she and Charlie sat down on the boat's bench again, they both stretched out their arms and basked in the glow of the sun. After they were quiet for a bit, Luna couldn't help returning to the conversation they'd started earlier. Like he'd said, how much could they talk about the weather? Curiosity toward one another was natural. "Explain to me, what is your exact purpose for this week with the M Dating Agency?"

"Tom advised that I've become intolerable. Apparently a CEO who works night and day but rarely sees his staff in person, doesn't remarry or at least date, who attends shareholder dinners and meetings via video, is problematic."

"I suppose that makes sense. They want to know you're flesh and blood, and not a myth." For her, it was the other way around.

"Ghost is more like it."

He said that so matter-of-factly Luna winced. His loss was unfathomably sad. "That you've accomplished all you have is a testament to your devotion."

After he seemed to stifle the thoughts Luna wished he'd have voiced, he continued, "I agreed with Tom that I'd start leaving the house more."

"Which, naturally, begins with a week in the company of a stranger in a mysterious destination not of your choosing?"

He let out a belly laugh so robust it drowned out the sound of the boat's motor. It was a laugh that she hoped to hear from him again this week, selfishly, because she adored the sound of it. "In a roundabout way, yes. Since I met you yesterday, these are certainly the most words I've said to another human in probably a year's time. I need to work on my social skills."

"Ironic that the man who needs to talk

more was paired with a woman who gets paid to speak."

"Yes. I've been wondering how Madison goes about making her matches."

They each opened a bottle of ice cold water and sipped. He was here to gear up to move forward. So was she, but forward to what? It was more like returning to something. To LA. To that life that had almost dragged her down to the bottom of the ocean, where she didn't think she'd ever breathe oxygen or see daylight again. Thank goodness she had gotten help in time.

The strangeness of this trip took hold of her, made her tense up. What on earth was she doing here with a man she'd just met? Was she ready? Yet maybe there was safety in this situation. Maybe she was to have this short interlude with Charlie, and then they'd go their separate ways, continents apart, and never encounter each other again.

She was so attracted to him. It was a giddy and alien sensation. She could imagine leaning over and kissing his full pale lips. Tucking herself into that outstretched arm and feeling the strength of his embrace. Further still, she envisioned sharing that sprawling bed at the villa with him, where they could be naked in the truest sense of the word, unbridled, uncensored, unselfconscious.

Charlie finally interrupted the silence. "What is it that you're here trying to *get over*?"

Even though she wanted to tell him everything, she chose to tell him nothing.

After the day on the water, Charlie and Luna returned to their villa and showered. They reconvened on the front patio, where cushy lounge chairs beckoned them to relax and watch the setting sun from their private beach.

"Chef Diego inquired whether we want him to bring dinner or if we'd enjoy cooking with him," Charlie said, reporting the message he'd received.

"That sounds nice, actually." She raked her fingers through her still-wet hair. The golden locks tumbled down from her scalp with bends and swirls. For the first time, it occurred to him why hair was described as wavy. Luna's mimicked the motion of the waves, which struck him as amazing. She looked so lovely stretched out on the lounger, with the long legs and pointed toes of a dancer. There was something profound about her organic beauty, a testament to the heavens. Charlie hadn't paid much attention to the attractiveness, or lack thereof, of the women around him. Because, frankly, there hadn't been many. An occasional AMgen employee who'd catch his eye, or someone from the mansion staff. But, overall, he'd been deadened to the charms of the female gender. He feared Luna had awoken a sleeping titan.

"Do you cook?" he asked, to get his mind off those shapely legs, which were on display given the short dress she'd put on.

"No."

"Never?"

"My mom has been cooking for me in Kentucky. In Los Angeles, I use a food delivery service. Three meals and two snacks arrive daily, all very organized."

"We mere mortals sometimes hear stories about the catering services on film sets overflowing with food and drinks all day and night during shoots."

"Oh, that's real. And the endless discussion and gossip about who ate what and how much. It's a badge of honor. The less you eat."

"The less you eat. There was a time in history when the more you ate was the status symbol."

"It's ridiculous. The press reporting on someone looking *relaxed* or *robust* or having a *new style*—all just thinly veiled code meaning they've gained weight."

"It must take special skills to have everyone's eyes on you all of the time."

"It messes with your mind. It did with mine, anyway."

"What an enormous amount of strain that must be."

"Senor and senorita, how was your day?" Chef Diego arrived in a golf cart and parked it next to the one Charlie had been driving. "Did you see many beautiful fish today?"

"It was spectacular, thank you," Luna replied with a smile as she swung her silky legs over the side of the lounger and rose. Charlie stood, as well. They watched as the chef unloaded his wheeled cart with the provisions he'd brought. They entered the villa, and Charlie was still surprised that he was staying in a structure without exterior walls. He'd felt no need to activate the glass enclosures, as the climate was delightful and, obviously, in their gated, private piece of paradise they didn't need to worry about intruders.

The three convened in the gourmet kitchen. "With your permission, tonight may I prepare for you Puerto Rico's official cocktail, the piña colada?"

Charlie and Luna looked at each other, her blue eyes twinkling. "Please," he answered.

They watched as the chef loaded pineapple juice, chunks of fresh pineapple, coconut cream, both dark and light rum and ice into a blender. "My personal touch," he explained as he squeezed in some lime. After whirling it into a thick, frosty emulsion, he poured it into shapely tall glasses, then garnished each with a triangle of pineapple and served them. *"Con gusto."*

"Deliciosa. The sweet and the cold are so good together," Luna exclaimed. "It's a vacation in a glass." Her tongue flicked the top of her lip to grab a drop, the movement not lost on Charlie. He stunned himself with his next thought. What it might be like to perform that lip-licking duty himself. And maybe to put a bit of the icy drink onto Luna's no-doubt warm skin, perhaps behind her ear and drink it off as it melted. Was he going crazy? He never, ever, had

thoughts like that. What was Puerto Rico doing to him?

"With your approval, tonight we will prepare one of the island's best-known dishes, *mofongo*."

"That's with *chicharrón* and green plantains?" Luna asked.

"Senorita, you've tasted it before?"

"No, I read about it in one of the magazines on the coffee table."

The three of them chuckled.

"Senor, I'll give you the honor of peeling the plantains and slicing them." The chef passed Charlie a cutting board and a knife. "These look like bananas, but the taste is much different," he said as he handed Charlie a bunch of the fruit. The skin was tough and thick. After peeling, Charlie began slicing them into disks.

"Senorita, if you'll heat the olive oil in the skillet."

Once they'd fried and drained the plantains, Chef Diego presented them with a mortar and pestle. "We call this a *pilón*. We will mash the plantains with the *chicharrón*, and garlic, and a little broth, as needed." The chef began placing chicken strips onto a sizzling grill. "*Chicharrón* are pork rinds that have been fried and seasoned."

Luna began the mashing, seeming to enjoy the task. "What's the history of this recipe?"

"Ah, good question. We believe it is an adaptation of the West African dish, *fufu*. Often you will see *mofongo* served in a rounded half-sphere shape. So we'll use these bowls as our mold." He showed them the glazed clay bowls.

"Why that shape?"

"As we tamp the *mofongo* into the bowl, we're going to scoop out the center and fill that with the grilled chicken. Then we will unmold it and surround it with hot broth, and as you eat you discover the chicken inside. Various fillings can be used."

Charlie was getting hungry from the descriptions and aromas. Once the *mofongo* was finished, the chef departed, and he and Luna took their plates to the courtyard again, as there could hardly be a lovelier place than under the twilight sky.

They also brought out the platter of fresh fruit that had been provided and the *arroz con dulce*, Puerto Rican rice pudding resplendent with raisins and spices.

As they ate, Luna regaled him with stories about other exotic destinations she'd been to. Charlie had traveled plenty himself for work, but chitchat didn't come as easily to him, so he appreciated her keeping the mood light while they ate. It was as if all of the years in his self-imposed isolation had caught up with him. There had been so much sorrow and anguish, so much grief and stabbing pain, that he'd forgotten there were other emotions. Being with Luna it registered how truly lonely he was.

CHAPTER FOUR

"WOULD YOU LIKE to go for a swim?" Luna asked once they'd finished their dinner. Old habits forced her through a mental process before she made the suggestion. It was dark now in the courtyard by their private pool. Charlie might be able to make out the outline of her body, but no one was going to pass judgment on her figure.

Even though they'd been out on the water snorkeling earlier, she'd quickly shrugged off her cover-up before they'd dove in and, likewise, slipped it right back on when they were done. It was frustrating that her brain had drudged her through all of those calculations, but as she'd learned in therapy, they were merely floating thoughts. While she couldn't seem to stop them, they didn't have to have any power over her unless she let them.

"That would be…nice." Charlie sounded tentative. But it was too early to go to bed and they hadn't made any other plans for the evening.

They cleared the plates and put everything on the cart, which Charlie wheeled to outside of the villa entrance as arranged. That way none of the staff would come through during the night, and a new cart with breakfast would be magically delivered in the morning.

"I'll just go get changed," Luna said and headed for the bedroom. Luckily, she'd brought several swimsuits. All modest one-pieces, of course. No bikinis for her. She threw on one of the terry-cloth robes with the Dorada logo that had been provided and belted it around her. Back outside, there was a cabinet filled with fresh towels near the pool.

Charlie strode out in swim trunks and nothing else. While he talked about his social awkwardness and she'd noticed that conversation with him could be choppy, he didn't seem to have any physical inhibitions. Lucky him, she thought.

She tossed her robe onto a chair and they got quickly into the pool. He dipped under the water and came back up, his hair dripping. "Ah, good idea, senorita."

"Muchas gracias."

She swam to the far end of the pool and he met her there, and then together they swam back. It was so relaxing to take lazy strokes, one after the other, like a moving meditation. Anush had been right—this getaway was what she needed. An escape with nothing that needed her attention. Except for a developing problem. A six-foot, green-eyed problem that was moving through the water next to her. Because after a day on the snorkeling boat and then cooking and eating with him, she was enjoying Charlie's company far more than she ought to.

This week was meant to include as much pretending as one of the films she'd acted in. Part of Anush's impetus was to help Luna prepare to date again, but she'd sworn she wasn't going to waste her time on the losers and users she tended to meet. In any case, she'd have her hands full reestablishing herself in LA. Dating wasn't going to be in the picture anytime soon.

For Charlie, he'd be going home to his English estate, hopefully with the spirit he'd need to socialize more, maybe date. This week was a sort of warm-up for both of them. She needed to cancel out the already developing feeling that it was going to be hard to say goodbye to him.

They swam to a bench in the pool, where they sat and looked up to the moon in the star-filled sky. "Did you know Luna means moon in Spanish?" she asked softly.

"Are you of Spanish descent?"

"No. My mom just heard it and thought it was pretty."

"Like you." The world deemed her pretty, too. If she was wearing the right outfit and had the right makeup and hair and so on. Somehow, though, Charlie saying so touched her. A smile crept across her mouth.

"What were you doing in Kentucky for a year?" he asked, not allowing for any meaningless blather.

"I—I got so far away from myself that I couldn't see my way back."

His eyes met hers in a direct stare. Now it was him who wanted to say something, but he seemed to be having trouble getting it out. "Yes," he whispered, as if he couldn't articulate more. His words echoed hers. "I know the feeling of not being able to see my way back."

Their faces inched closer together as they sat on the bench in the pool. Were they about to kiss? In an instant, she wanted to. More than anything in the world. One inch closer still, and their eyes stayed joined in a lifeline. The intensity was almost too much to bear. He was hesitating. Maybe she should make the first move. Tilting her head slightly, she leaned in.

She saw the arch in his shoulders as his back stiffened. His body language was clear. If she had thought the swell of yearning for each other was mutual, she'd been very wrong.

It was another long night of lying on the sofa, staring out of the villa at the night sky, but with sleep not coming. This time, Charlie had so much on his mind it was no wonder slumber eluded him. Luna had tried to kiss him in the swimming pool after dinner. What's more, he had most certainly wanted to kiss her back. To claim her tender lips and feel them move under his. To hear a catch of desire in her breath. The mere thought of that made his blood run scalding hot. It had been a decade. Ten long years, during which he'd scarcely even thought of intimacies with another woman, and never imagined that was something he'd ever have again. He assumed that was in the past for him. As if his hormonal system, his entire sexuality, had died along with his wife.

It was a subconscious reaction to lean away when it seemed a kiss with Luna was looming. Nothing like that was supposed to happen between them and he was glad he didn't act on the moment. It was too sudden, too shocking. But he couldn't stop ruminating over it. Welcome or not, Luna was digging up the mental and emotional grave he'd been buried in.

Quite early in the morning, Madison Morgan called, thankfully ending his restless night. "Charlie, I'm calling to inquire how things are going. Did the bed arrangement settle itself out?"

"We're sleeping separately, as intended."

"For now."

Charlie could only nod to himself at her single-mindedness. Sadly, he'd be proving her wrong but he was curious. "Can I ask you something? How do you go about matching people up?"

"That's my own secret formula, Charlie. As a mastermind, I'm sure you understand."

"Still, I wonder why you chose Luna and I as a pair?"

"Your question tells me you should leave your intellect in your luggage and just let things flow for the week."

"If you've done your work to know me at all, you'd know that's not in my character."

"Exactly, Charlie. Exactly." And with that, Madison ended the call. Charlie sank farther into the cocoon of the sofa where he'd spent the night replayed Madison's words.

"Hello," Luna called out softly when the sun had moved higher in the sky. Charlie rose and ran his fingers through his hair. She appeared in a long beach dress made of a golden fabric. With her hair as flowing as the garment, she was a mystical vision from the heavens. A throb in his loins made him feel like an animal. It was an exhilarating, virile sensation. He liked it.

"Let me get the cart with our breakfast," he said and hurried to the entrance, wanting to be the provider.

"Thank you," she replied ever so sweetly as he wheeled it in. A vase filled with flowers adorned the breakfast offerings.

After coffee, they dug in to the selections, and the ubiquitous and welcome tray of fresh-cut fruit. If she'd been upset by his unwillingness to kiss her last night, she didn't let it show. Then again, she was an actress, after all. "What would you like to do today?" He grabbed his tablet, ready to punch in their requirements.

"Another day on the water, perhaps? I'd like to try paddleboarding."

"Your wish is my command." With a couple of taps, he organized it so that someone would meet them at the shoreline with the equipment.

"And let's have the chef just deliver our dinner. Whatever he chooses. We had enough food decisions to make yesterday."

Soon enough they were at the waterfront. As they were both novices, a Dorada staff member named Martino, who was dressed in shorts and a polo shirt with the resort's insignia, gave them a few tips. He showed them how to use the paddles, and they practiced until they had the feel for it. Then they kneeled on their boards and headed away from the beach as Martino left.

"Do you want to try kneeling, sitting, lying prone, or standing?" Charlie said, keeping his board as near to Luna's as he could.

"I want to stand."

He did, too, but he also wanted to watch as Luna stood first. He felt better able to assist her if she needed it from where he was. As instructed, from her kneeling position she brought up one knee to her chest and flattened her foot on the board, then repeated the action with the other. With that stance, she was able to stand fully erect and stabilize herself. A huge smile spread across her face. "I did it!" Her enthusiasm was infectious, so Charlie repeated the same steps, until he stood tall on his own board. "Once you get the hang of keeping your balance you can just look out to the horizon while you paddle."

"It's marvelous." Charlie could hardly believe himself. From a mansion with dark heavy curtains he rarely drew open to walking on water with a gorgeous companion in the Caribbean. He couldn't be further from his norm. He was beginning to wonder which one was him, and who he wanted to be. Amelia wouldn't have liked what he'd become over the last decade. An outsider. A loner. Without excitement, without joy. He thought he owed his endless mourning to her and Lily, as a testament of his love for them. But walking in the memorial garden he'd planted for them on the estate's grounds was often the only time he saw sunlight. They deserved better than that from him.

They coasted quietly, both soaking in the sea and sun. Neither noticed an unexpected rough wave coming toward them. "Yikes!" Luna exclaimed and was promptly knocked off her board by its force. Her board skidded to one side, her paddle toward Charlie. He was able to squat and grab it.

Luna tumbled under the water, tossed by the undertow. Charlie kneeled to speed up his paddling, racing to get to her before the situation became perilous. The water wasn't terribly deep but he didn't want her to get hurt. He was able to reach his arm to her and sighed with relief when he felt her hand grab it and clutch on to him.

Anguish stabbed into him. The arm he gave Luna was the figurative arm he had never been able to extend to his wife and baby. Intellectually, Charlie knew there was nothing he could have done to prevent the accident that took away the world as he knew it. He hadn't even been there. But that didn't stop him from being haunted by the fact that he hadn't been able to save them.

He hoisted up Luna until she could get her knees balanced on his board. "All you all right?" he asked right away to be sure.

"Oh, yeah." She laughed. "I guess we're beginners, after all. We should have seen that coming. Wait, are you okay?"

"Why wouldn't I be?"

"You're the one who looks white as a ghost."

"Thank you. That was very noble of you to react so quickly," Luna said to Charlie a bit later, as they were lying on a blanket atop the sand. She'd been surprised that Charlie looked so shaken after she'd taken the tumble off her paddleboard. "Thankfully, I'm a fairly competent swimmer."

Had he been afraid for her safety because he'd come to care about her in the short time they'd known each other? It was a charming notion, but she doubted it. Her potential peril tapped into something else in him, that much was obvious.

"I suppose in Los Angeles, you're in swimming pools and the Pacific Ocean quite a bit?"

"When I get the chance. I had been working a lot before my hiatus." Charlie handed her a cold bottle of tangerine soda from their picnic basket along with an assortment of seasoned nuts in a container. "Although *hiatus* is a polite word for what I did."

"You said Los Angeles had become too much for you."

"When I fled to Kentucky, I was two days from beginning a new film. I violated my contract and left a lot of people in the lurch."

"You said you were due to start another film after this week in Puerto Rico."

"Yes."

"So your reputation wasn't ruined to the point that people didn't want to work with you." She nodded her head, appreciating the support. Charlie Matthews might be a sad man, but he was a kind one at the same time.

She couldn't help recalling last night in the swimming pool. When she'd almost kissed him. It felt so right until, in the blink of an eye, it felt so wrong. And now those impulses were moving through her again. Pulling her toward him. She'd be lying if she didn't admit that his assist when she was swept off the paddleboard had been welcome, even if she didn't need it. No man had ever really cared for her well-being.

"True," she replied, agreeing with Charlie's assessment that her career hadn't been irrevocably damaged by her sudden departure, as the reason was purposely never explained to the parties involved. "I've done a great job of hiding my feelings for years."

"That's the spirit."

At that she chuckled, and Charlie did, as well.

"I suppose it'll be good to get back to work. This next one is an action blockbuster film. I play the love interest to the main superhero."

He shook his head back and forth. "This is terrible to admit to you, but I don't line up to see those big-event movies when they're released. I can report, though, that half of London does. They buy advance tickets and merchandise and create a frenzy. From a business standpoint, it's quite a phenomenon."

"And made me very wealthy. I'll tell you, though, someday I'd like to make more personal movies about ordinary women with real-life super powers."

"I'm sure you will." Another vote of confidence from him. Luna had better watch herself. A billionaire who had nothing to gain by sucking up to see what he could get from her could be a risky attraction. She didn't want to leave Puerto Rico with a broken heart.

Once the afternoon sun had lowered and they'd had their fill of mastering paddleboarding, they returned to the villa and showered. On a whim, Luna put on a slinky silver dress with spaghetti straps. She'd normally throw a scarf or light cardie over it, because every inch of her body she'd ever revealed ended up as someone else's concern, so she'd learned to cover up. Not that something as simple as a pashmina stopped the scrutiny, but at least they weren't discussing her skeleton. Tonight she was feeling comfortable enough around Charlie that she didn't feel the need to cover up.

The way those brilliant green eyes took her in when she emerged from the bedroom was all the validation she needed. Around him, she was the least self-conscious she'd ever been. She'd had only the briefest fleeting thoughts about her body when they were paddleboarding, which was huge progress for her. "You are, er, enchanting," he stut-

tered out, all the more adorable because
he was awkward with the compliment. He
looked awfully good himself in a black shirt
not tucked into the jeans that were snug
around his muscular legs.

They sat down in the dining room to eat
the dinner Chef Diego had left them. *Pollo
guisado* was a delicious spicy chicken stew.
Dessert was a small chocolate cake in the
shape of a heart, adorned with candied ed-
ible rose petals. The sight of the cake caused
a catch in Luna's throat. That was a cake for
lovers to share. The staff would have no way
of knowing that she and Charlie were here
for what could only be described as self-
improvement. In a way, for Luna it was the
culmination of her treatment.

As she looked at the cake, she said, "I want
to tell you about Kentucky." She needed to
expose herself to him. To voice the words
that she'd kept secret for so long. Doing so
would cement her recovery. And he was the
perfect person to talk to. A CEO with his
own problems who lived half a world away
from her. Someone she'd never see again
after this brief interlude together.

"Okay."

"As I was expressing to you before, issues around appearance and perfection are common in my world. In order to compete, which is what it sometimes feels like, I had started to restrict the food I ate. Obsessing on it, really. It took me over."

His brow furrowed with concern. "It's unfortunate it went that far."

"Yes, it definitely snowballed when the paparazzi started to comment on how much weight I'd lost—positively of course, saying how enviably slim I was. In reality, though, my body weight had dropped so low that I hardly had the energy to get out of bed every day."

"Ugh," he growled, "disgusting that anyone would make *your* body *their* business at all."

"And then it reached a breaking point when I man I was dating, Troy Lutt, took some photos of me when I was at my lowest weight and sold them to the tabloids."

"I'd like to wring his neck."

"Yes, it taught me that people will sink to unimaginable levels for their own gain."

"Luna, I can't even fathom how horrible that must have been for you."

"I couldn't function. And yet the press ran those pictures as if I looked great. When I saw them, I knew I was looking at someone very ill, even though that's not what the world saw. I didn't want to put a name on my problem. I just wanted to consider it an occupational hazard that I'd be able to handle."

"Did you?"

"No. Thank goodness for my stylist, Anush, who, over the years, has become my best friend. The more she tried to point out that it had become an issue, the more I tried to push her away. I kept my family at a distance, too, but they knew. Anush kept on it, though, until I had to admit that I needed outside help."

"Thank you, Anush, whoever you are."

"She assisted me in arranging everything. A recovery program that wasn't far from my parents' ranch in Kentucky. My mom and dad were supportive and grateful that I was able to get professional support in time."

"And now?"

Luna took a breath before she answered. "I completed an intensive program for treatment of anorexia nervosa." There, she'd said the words out loud. The medical diagnosis. "I can now recognize triggers before they cause me to take regrettable actions. It's something I'll have to manage for the rest of my life but I know I can do it. We don't know each other but you'll have to believe me when I tell you that I wouldn't have been able to sit here and enjoy a meal a year ago."

"Thank you for sharing something so intimate with me, Luna."

It was incredibly liberating to tell the story to someone outside of her bubble. It had been a dark road she traversed, but she'd made it to the light. She felt bare but enormously relieved. Her adrenaline was running, giving her the courage to try again what she'd started last night in the pool. This time, when gravity brought their faces together, neither of them withdrew. Instead, they allowed their lips to meet, touching and then leaning away, touching and then leaning away. Her eyelashes fluttered uncontrollably. And then their lips parted and their tongues mingled, and Luna swooned under Charlie's kiss.

CHAPTER FIVE

"I NEED TO come up for air," Luna said as she removed her arms from around Charlie's neck after they'd been kissing for several minutes. Her move threw him into disorientation, so captivated had he been by her soft lips. She brushed her hair back off her face and swallowed hard. "I haven't kissed someone like that in a long time."

"I'll bet it's been longer for me than it has for you," he said as he brought the back of his hand across his mouth as if to wipe off what had just happened.

"You haven't been with anyone since your wife died?"

"Absolutely not." After the first year, old friends and colleagues had tried to fix him up with women they knew. Said it was healthy for him. He politely refused every time and they'd eventually given up. The loss of his beloved wife and child had left him not even curious about dating again. Amelia was the only woman for him. Now, at thirty-two, he was finally open to questioning his self-imposed exile. Charlie had even felt the spirit of Amelia come to him in the darkest hours of torturous nights and tell him that he needed more than what he'd whittled his life down to. "That was part of the impetus for this week with the M Agency. To remember how to socialize again."

"For me, too."

He had to admit to himself that he smarted with rejection when she'd broken the kiss. Before his brain had a chance to say no, he'd gotten lost in the pillowy sensation of her full lips on his, each of his hands on either side of her face. "I've forgotten what kissing like that felt like."

"So, what did it feel like?"

"Good. Dangerously good." He was grateful for the smile that admission brought, lightening the awkwardness of the moment. "Just for my education, did I kiss you or did you kiss me?"

"I believe it was mutual."

"I don't think it can be mutual. One person has to make that final move to initiate contact."

"I think it was you."

"No, I think it was you." Another welcome chuckle.

"Shall we agree to disagree?"

"And make a pact to be sure it doesn't happen again?" That fell out of Charlie's mouth as natural as day. Really, he was getting the sense he might like to do a lot more kissing of Luna's succulent mouth. And not just her mouth, either. Those inklings had been so suppressed in him, he could hardly believe that they were surfacing. Yet they were. Things were moving too fast. Maybe it was, in fact, time he opened to dating again. To sharing touch, physical intimacy. But it would be a slow process. This week was meant only to slip the key into the lock. He wasn't ready for the gates to open.

She'd probably experienced a tiny jolt of rebuff by his suggestion. That was okay. Better a little misunderstanding now than something much bigger later. "Of course," she murmured.

Revealing her eating disorder to him couldn't have been easy. He couldn't begin to understand what that agony must have been like for her. He hoped she wouldn't think that had anything to do with him suggesting that they didn't tempt fate with any more physical contact. "Not that I don't find you extremely attractive." He was hopeless, making a mess of his words.

"No, I understand. It was a moment. It's passed."

All squared away then. So why was Charlie at full-on war with his arms, which were fighting to wrap themselves around Luna's shoulders again? Eager to reinitiate the splendid meeting of their lips and tongues joined in that merging that made the world around him melt away. To bring his lips to her elegant neck, to the divot between her breasts that he bet smelled as fragrant as the flowers of the island. To take his mouth further still, into the secrets of her very being.

That he was in close company with a woman at all was hard to fathom. He'd so forgotten the pure charm of a woman, the fundamental differences that completed yin to yang, Adam to Eve. How Luna moved, with a limber slink that struck him as inherently feminine. How unspeakably soft her skin was. And what she was stirring inside of him—a primordial pull toward her, making him want to be both predator and protector at the same time. Was he ready for an awakening? Was it the right thing to do?

At last, he refocused enough to ask a question. "You've said your dating life has been under scrutiny as much as your appearance?"

"Oh." She cleared her throat. "Yes, the paparazzi are almost as interested in who I'm seen with as they are with what I'm wearing. I go out with men who are in the entertainment industry that I've met on set, or sometimes my team matches me up with someone else who is single. Like Troy. My *publicist* fixed me up with him and then he embarrassed me publicly. There's irony for you."

Charlie wasn't able to understand what Luna's life was like. Evenings spent with men she didn't even know. Is that what he was supposed to be doing with new women? "Do you find that you get along with them?"

"I can pass an evening with someone. Invariably, they're looking to leverage being seen with me to further their own careers. The whole thing is riddled with insincerity."

"I'd imagine so." He studied her again, wondering if this rich and famous and troubled woman longed for basic things, like genuine love. Children. Like what he used to have. "Have you ever really cared about anyone you've dated?"

"To be honest, no. Very few people look at me and really see who I am inside. Like I told you, they see Luna Price. A thing. A commodity."

If he was with her, he thought, he'd show her every day that he cared about her. The woman, not the image. She deserved that much. What a strange predicament her life must be. No wonder she'd developed unhealthy behaviors.

In a natural sync, they brought the plates into the kitchen. He was still recounting the kisses they'd shared, and thought he might for the rest of his life. They'd been smart enough to recognize that they'd acted on impulse and wouldn't do it again. It was best not to confuse their intentions for the week. Still, he was reeling. It was more than just the possibility of opening up to a woman again, after he thought he never would, that had him in tumult. It was Luna specifically—she was reaching down into his soul with her own truth, which was terrifying in its starkness.

"It's nice to have this time with you, Charlie."

"Is it?"

She gave him a questioning look. Had he said the wrong thing again? "I'm going to bed. Good night."

"Good night, Luna."

Before she left the kitchen she lifted up on tiptoes to plant a silky peck on his cheek. As he watched her walk away, he bought up his hand to the exact spot that was radiating from where her sweet lips had touched it.

Charlie watched as Luna lean back and took a sip of her juice. It was another picture-perfect morning in their private courtyard. Equally scenic was his beautiful companion, in a gauzy dress that hid nothing of her lanky physique, all planes and angles. The unplanned kisses they'd shared last night hadn't lost their prominent place front and center in his mind.

"What does the company name AMgen represent?" She folded up one knee, pretzeling herself in the chair, and probably didn't realize how provocative that looked. The twitchy response in his center was proof.

"The AM is for Amelia. And gen, as in

generation, innovation. I was a young man when I started the company."

"You married young, too."

"Amelia and I were schoolmates. We were together from the time we were teenagers. Married at nineteen, poor as dirt. We used the little bit of money we got as wedding gifts from relatives to start AMgen in a tiny office on Old Street in London. Amelia ran things and kept the books."

"And look at your company now."

"She grew up with nothing, raised by a single mother. I told her I'd give her everything she could ever dream of, and that our children wouldn't want for anything. That I'd be bold, take my ideas as far as they could go."

"The business grew quickly?"

"Yes. Every bit of money I made, I put back in. I was able to hire more employees and lease large office space. An unheard of ascension for someone my age, really. Then Amelia had a wobbly pregnancy so she stopped working in order to rest. When Lily was born, we were on cloud nine. We had it all."

He felt a veil of stone weigh down his face, even under Luna's compassionate watch. His had been an idyllic story to tell. Until the tragedy. Until the part that turned everything upside down. Until what was important was stolen away by a thief in the night.

"Charlie, I'm so sorry your happiness didn't last forever."

"It was a car accident at Christmastime. The roads were slick and icy. Amelia and the baby had been returning from a visit to her mother's house." He'd replayed the story endlessly, told it to countless psychologists and counselors in the beginning. It never got easier. "I was at home at the time. It was a trip she'd taken a hundred times, even in winter weather."

An exhale whooshed out of him. Would the gruesome details ever recede into the distance?

"Go on."

"The driver of the other car had an excessive amount of alcohol in her system. Slammed into Amelia's car at a high speed. My wife and baby were killed instan—" He couldn't finish the sentence. He didn't need to.

Luna got up from her chair and went to him. Such an unfamiliar gesture, yet he was grateful for an offer of affection. Still sitting, he wrapped his arms around her waist and pressed his face into the side of her hip. The loneliness he'd emotionally stifled for so many years beat within him. Sorrow overtook him. Perhaps the floodgates had opened a bit after last night, when Luna told him about her own deep struggles. She combed her fingers through his hair. Her pure and gentle consideration was a salve. Neither spoke for a long while.

"So, you see," he finally said when his breathing flowed clearly again, "I want to uphold my promise to my wife and child, to continue to grow, to challenge, to lead. I'll do whatever it takes. It's my way of keeping them alive. I'll never remarry or love again."

Luna sat propped up on pillows in the middle of the gigantic bed in the master suite. A beach-read novel lay on one side of her, the script for her next film on the other. She wanted to review her lines. Her phone and the TV remote controls were scattered on the bed, as well. The large flat-screen on the wall ran a sitcom without sound.

Earlier, in the courtyard, she'd witnessed a drama far more powerful than anything her profession could have produced. No movie, symphony, painting or any other art form could have expressed the gravity of raw emotion she'd seen when Charlie told her about the death of his wife and child. From the minute she'd met him, the suffering behind his green eyes was evident. Only now, she knew the exact specifics of why. As he recounted the early days of his marriage and the forming of his company, it was as if invisible bullets were shooting through him. He contracted here and there, jerked this way and that as he told the story with tiny, almost unperceivable movements that hadn't been unnoticed by her.

Afterward, she'd moved toward him on impulse, compelled by his pain to want to comfort him. Human to human, with no motive or forethought. It was the least she could do, the right thing to do. He'd clutched her tightly for a short moment, needing her as a pillar, as she'd guessed he might. Quickly enough, though, he finished and dropped his arms. Had he made himself too vulnerable? Or was it that the burden of grief he'd been carrying for ten years already knew only to rear itself in short bursts? Afterward, he said he was tired and wanted to rest a bit, a late-morning siesta. Alone in *his* portion of the villa, of course.

She imagined him stretched out on the luxurious sofa he'd claimed as his bed. *Hmm*, she thought with a wry smile, *did the sofa know how lucky it was to have him on top of it?* Those explosive kisses they'd *accidentally* shared still ricocheted through her. The power of his lips, coveting her, ushering her into a haze she didn't want to wake from. A yearning pulsed within her. Today, as he spoke of his undying love for his wife and baby, a longing she had never recognized began bouncing around in her.

Sprawling back on the pillows, Luna watched the ceiling fan swirl. The devotion he had described was nothing she'd ever known. Maybe she actually did hope for a man to love her, and whom she could love back. She was twenty-eight years old. It was time she made some decisions. What would it be like to have mutual admiration and respect with someone? To give and to receive. To hold one up when the other was down and vice versa. For someone else's best interests to be hers. That she'd been able to confide in Charlie about the anorexia felt like an enormous step. What would it be like to further share burdens with someone, along with joys?

CHAPTER SIX

LUNA'S PHONE BUZZED. "It's Madison Morgan. I'm checking in to see how things are going."

"It's unusual to be in such romantic surroundings when neither of us are here looking for anything ongoing." She surely didn't need to tell the matchmaker about the ups and downs and intimate forays that had already occurred.

"And you're absolutely sure about that?"

"Yes." She answered definitively even though she was no longer sure at all. "I'm here to reset on what's important. And Charlie is here to get comfortable being out there in the world."

"You know all about that, Luna. Help him out."

She didn't exactly understand what Madison was talking about, but somehow Luna pictured her as a fortune-teller wearing a turban and staring into a crystal ball.

Later that day, Luna decided to give Charlie a little visual demonstration of her public skills. Maybe Madison was right—that was something she could help him with.

"I'm Charlie Matthews. Who are you?" he joked when she sashayed into the living room. Still lounging on the sofa, he sat right up and rubbed his eyes with the heels of his hands.

"I told you. When I put *her* on, she's like a whole different person."

"You look positively…untouchable." When he paused, she'd thought he was going to pay her a compliment, but his tone was anything but complimentary.

"This is what the public and the press want to see. I'm larger than life," she exclaimed with a toss of her hair. "Supposedly some kind of aspiration."

"Uh-huh?"

She had given herself a head-to-toe Luna Price makeover before she exited the bedroom. "Let me take you on a tour from top to bottom." She sauntered to him with an exaggerated sway to her hips and zhooshed her hair with a widespread palm. "First, the hair is blown out with a handheld dryer. Next comes a straightening iron for sleekness. Then a curling iron for *unnatural* natural waves."

"But your hair is already wavy, isn't it? Or at least it has been for the last couple of days. Why would you straighten it to curl it?" Shirtless on the sofa with his own hair tousled, she had to get her focus off how sexy he looked in order to continue.

"Yes, but *actual* natural waves can't be relied upon, dah-ling. What if there was humidity in the air?" She picked up a lock and twirled it around her finger. "Or one curl was out of place? Disaster of epic proportions, don't you know?"

"I see." He smiled at her cheekiness.

Charlie's jaw had all but dropped open at her display. She wanted to cheer him up from the suffering he'd told her about over the last couple of days. Plus, if he was ready to date again, he'd probably be interacting with glamorous women befitting his billionaire status. Truth be told, she wanted to put herself to the test, as well. Had she really learned to put that self-awareness about her body in a proper place, where it wouldn't cause her so much pain? Was she ready to go back to stardom and the responsibilities that entailed? And was there a chance she could juggle that while relating honestly to a man?

Charlie fixed his gaze on her face, squinting to study the trickery she'd applied with a chemist's skill.

"Foundation makeup, administered so thoroughly that there isn't a spec of my face that hasn't been smoothed over until flawless."

"You're already flawless."

If she wasn't wearing so much makeup he might have seen her blush. "Eyeliner, several shades of eye shadow chosen from a complementary color palette, false eyelashes and a half gallon of mascara give my eyes that smoky look ready to attract anything they survey." She turned away from him, then snapped her neck sideways so she could shoot him a slit-eyed smoldering gaze over her shoulder. He fell backward onto the sofa as if he'd been shot. They both laughed.

She returned to her tutorial, gesturing to her face. "Brows have been enhanced. Bronzer added back the glow to my skin that the Puerto Rican sunshine had given me—"

"But the makeup had taken away," he interrupted.

"Wonderful. You're learning."

"Fascinating."

She mimed applying lipstick. "Lip liner followed by lipstick followed by lip gloss."

"So they'll be no kissing?" *Gulp.* There it was, mention again of that mind-bending kissing over the heart-shaped cake they never ate. The kisses that weren't supposed to have happened but that she couldn't stop replaying.

Back to the task at hand. "Certainly not. Mess up this work of art?"

"Of course, never."

She ran a hand down the length of her body. "Makeup applied everywhere the clothes don't cover. Not a freckle, mole or mark shall mar this perfection."

"It's—it's not the makeup that's perfection," he stuttered adorably.

"Luna Price devoted herself to reaching fame and fortune," she began, using a documentarian's narration, as if she was describing a herd of wildlife. "From as far back as she could remember, little Luna wanted to perform. Her mother used to sing to her, instilling in Luna a wish to express herself.

Ruth Price had sung in school choirs and the high-school spring musicals, but lacked the confidence to pursue her interest professionally. Once young Luna had the same leanings, Ruth encouraged her to study acting and take seriously the talent she displayed."

"Hmm. How interesting."

"Next, what you don't see about the illusion." She continued her demonstration by grabbing a pinch of her dress and pulling it outward, just to let Charlie hear it snap back into place when she released it. "A secret undergarment from here—" she gestured under her bra line "—to here." She indicated above her knees. "That smooths and shapes me."

"What is that made of?"

"Something highly elasticized."

"Is that uncomfortable?"

"I can hardly breathe."

"Torture."

"But look." She curtsied. "No unsightly lumps or bulges."

"Aren't women intended to have lumps and bulges?"

"Not in Hollywood." It was fun not to take everything so seriously for a minute.

"Right."

"Luna's father, Jack, ran a small ranch. He was bemused by his daughter's playacting in the living room, and singing and dancing along to pop videos. Both Jack and Ruth only wanted their daughter to be happy, whatever road she chose."

"They sound like good people."

"Now, if you'll forgive me for being so personal, next comes a bra that basically begins pulling my skin upward from my knees in order to give me this—" she mimed cupping her own breasts "—cleavage. Inserted are silicone cutlets to add volume."

"So that's not all you?"

"Nope."

"Cutlets. What a term."

"And as you can plainly see, a simple black cocktail dress." She circled around to give him the full effect of the dress, which was skintight. Everywhere. "That costs more than some people make in a year."

"It's a little tube of black fabric."

"After earning a degree in drama from a state university," she went on, "Luna ventured to Los Angeles, like millions of other hopefuls, taking her shot at the limelight. She worked as a waitress, a delivery driver and at a cosmetics counter before she began to win small roles in films and television. With the help of a hardworking agent, scripts came her way and she was able to ascend to the top of her field."

"That's really remarkable. The odds must be one in a million."

His praise was different than what she heard from fans or read online; he acknowledged that she deserved everything that came to her. There was so much jealousy in LA. Yes, she'd had luck on her side but there had been many years of hard work.

"And finally—" she wiggled her fingers and then pointed downward "—constant manicures and pedicures. Deeming my feet worthy of stiletto sandals encrusted with Swarovski crystals."

"How can you walk in heels that high?"

"*Very* slowly. And on the arm of a beefy guy in a tuxedo for stability."

"I'm exhausted. How long does it take you to look like that?"

"A couple of hours. But worth it, no?"

"No."

She cocked her head in question.

"I mean, you're absolutely stunning," he explained. "No doubt about it. But..."

Oh. Was Charlie Matthews going to be

just like the crowd in Los Angeles? Always looking to find flaws?

"I only meant that, to tell you the truth, I can't imagine you looking any more beautiful than you do coming out of the shower in one of your beach dresses with your hair blown by the sea breeze and no makeup concealing your creamy skin."

Tears blinked in Luna's eyes. No one had ever told her that she looked beautiful without the Hollywood facade cloaking her every day. Since her career had taken off, she'd lived with that inch-by-inch examination of her from head to toe. That scrutiny had led her to a deadly relationship with nutrition, lest the naysayers find the imperfections they were looking for.

"Charlie," she said in a hushed tone with a bobble in her voice as she sat down beside him. "That's the nicest thing anyone has ever said to me."

Charlie didn't exactly understand why Luna looked like she was about to cry when he'd merely mentioned that she was prettier in her natural state before all of the piled-on enhancements she'd just demonstrated. He'd clearly pushed a sensitive button. "Well, you are fab-u-lous either way," he said, mimicking a glamorous voice to try to get her back into the jovial mood she came in with for her show and tell.

Dare he admit he was enjoying himself with her here on this weeklong adventure? They seemed to be able to quickly toggle from solemnity to silliness and then back again. To connect, really connect, with someone after so long was far more poignant than he expected it to be. Were he to return to England with the eventual goal of socializing with women, he wouldn't expect it to be a repeat of either the conviviality or the candor he was sharing with Luna. It was a fact that actually had him a bit worried.

While she did look glitzy in her movie-star makeup and dress, it was almost hard to reconcile her with the woman he'd been getting to know over the last few days. The Luna who was starting to mean something to him. Certainly Charlie had no intention of feeling for a woman ever again. Faded memories were all he'd held in his arms, and so it was to remain until he took his last breath. Perhaps this week was making him see that dinners and even physical intimacy might be possible again as long as they didn't touch his heart. Yet he was finding himself attached to Luna. Which could only bring him harm.

But the woman behind the lipstick was so alluring, he had an odd impulse to pull her onto his lap, wipe off all of the gunk and kiss her again like he had last night. To smell her fresh skin, not the perfume emanating off the makeup and hair products. To again burrow down into the authentic her, down to her soul. But these were more thoughts that were most definitely not part of the week's agenda.

A clench squeezed through his body at having her sitting beside him right now, he in only shorts that allowed the taut fabric of her fancy dress to brush against his bare leg. Having her in such close proximity was testing his will. He didn't like it and he liked it too much.

"All right. I just wanted to show you Luna Price in her full regalia. How about if I change back into something comfortable?"

He was curious how she'd even gotten into such an elaborate outfit all on her own. She was a pro, that's how. But he definitely found himself wondering about all of the undergarments she had described. Silicone

cutlets to enhance her breasts? In the swimsuits and leisure wear she'd worn while in
Puerto Rico, he'd had occasion, maybe
more than once, to glance at the outline of
her breasts. They were lovely and certainly
needed no augmentation. Other than his
hands holding them, that is.

Certainly, she should free herself from
the confining garment she had explained.
How did that work? he wondered. Did one
simply step into it and roll it up on the body,
then to emancipate from it, reverse the process? Why did it sound like a contraption
that might be better off being battery-oper-
ated? What about remote-controlled, so that
he could press a button and watch the piece
roll off Luna and he could see her glorious
body naked and uncontorted? He resisted
a smile at his own imagination. Maybe he
should get into complex women's undergarments as an AMgen expansion.

Next, he tried to picture the amount of
products it might take to remove all of the
heavy makeup she wore. Although those
fire-engine-red lips were a classic symbol
of female beauty, he longed to again see
the dusty rose of her undressed mouth. He
thought about washing her face himself, a

soapy cloth lathering away all of the obstacles to her radiance. Standing behind her in front of the mirror, he'd lightly move the cloth in circles around her face, using special gentleness around her eye area. Then, pressing himself into her from behind, he'd bend her forward over the sink so that he could rinse her face over and over again with warm water. When all of the facade had been washed away, he'd grab a fluffy towel to pat her face dry. Then she'd be naked in every sense of the word.

Envisioning all of that was causing a throb in his loins. A wake-up call to that entire part of himself that he hadn't explored in so very long, he was convinced it was gone. He was as afraid of it as much as he welcomed it, alarming in its absolute power. Confused, annoyed even, he got up, strode right through the villa, out to the courtyard, and dove straight into the deep end of the swimming pool without saying a word.

By the time he got out of the pool, Luna had washed up and changed into a T-shirt and skirt, and had brought food out to the courtyard. She sat at the table spearing her grilled seafood with pasta, having started eating while he was still swimming. Charlie's mood had soured during the swim. He'd gone from having that pleasant eroticism he'd experienced thinking about ridding Luna of that costume she'd put on, which had led him to want to cool off in the water, to now being brought back to the dark cellar where he usually spent his days. He joined her and chomped listlessly on the food, knowing he wasn't being good company.

Once he'd begun wallowing in his grief again, aware of the blood having drained from his pallor, he neither had anything to say nor the voice to say it in. Sure, he could lose himself in the work of designing new technologies for medical advances. Alone with ideas in his extensively equipped home office, he could envision, create and problem-solve. But remaining emotionally consistent out in the world was a science he no longer had any aptitude for.

These last few days with Luna had been frightening. Because he'd vowed to never, ever rely on anyone again. Most definitely never risk a loss so great it would swallow him alive for a second time. And now investors and shareholders were involved in his personal business? Was it up to them to decide that he should date or remarry?

Most unexpectedly, Luna had pulled on his heartstrings. Her honesty, intelligence and humor had brought a light to his eyes that he thought had been extinguished forever. In the wee hours, when he imagined Amelia coming to console and advise him, he never told her phantom that he was too scared to let love back in. Because what if it was snatched away again, as she and their beautiful baby had been? There was too much uncertainty. He couldn't make the leap of faith.

He did understand that his solitude wasn't healthy for him. So he needed to get through this week with Luna and then perhaps he'd ask an attractive coworker to dinner in London. Not someone like Luna, though, who was summoning dangerous feelings—dangerous because they were real.

"You're sad," she said, as if she could sense his distance.

"I suppose."

"That's okay." How gracious she was. Far more than he was.

What he didn't want to say was that being honest was too hard. And, for that matter, too unfamiliar. He'd spent the better part of ten years in silence. Sure, there was the discussion with the housekeeper about the bedsheets. There were powwows with Tom and the other high-ranking staffers at AMgen. But it was always about the business at hand. Tom had long tried to reach out to him but Charlie had kept him at bay.

He'd seen the grief specialists after Amelia and Lily were killed. Whether they had done him any good he couldn't say. Tragedy was tragedy. There was no silver lining, no looking on the bright side. Time didn't heal the wounds. Every absurd clichéd phrase of comfort had meant absolutely zero to him. A shadow of a man, he'd marched forward nonetheless, one foot in front of the next. And now he had the next battle, to save himself from running AMgen into the ground.

He stared out to the hedge that enclosed the courtyard. The foliage reminded him of the memorial flower garden he'd planted on his estate. He'd installed a stone bench engraved with the names of his wife and daughter, to replace the white lawn chairs that had been there. With his gardener's guidance, Charlie had planted the flowers on his own. On hands and knees, he'd dug into the soil himself. Stayed at it for hours, day after day, until it was done. There had been some catharsis in that. The dirt under his fingernails at night was an exhibition of his grief. He'd chosen over a dozen varieties so that there would be blooms year-round.

It was a spot where Amelia had liked to sit. Even now, it was his favorite place on his grand, lonely property. He still went there to think. To read. Symbolically, it had become the place he felt loved. He suddenly wished he was within its safety right now. The vibrant colors of Puerto Rico, along with the equally vibrant woman before him, were too much to take. He may have made a mistake in agreeing to this week.

Although, he remembered, Madison's policy was to donate a large amount of the fee she charged for her services to charities that her clients had chosen. That was one of the reasons she ran the M Dating Agency. There was at least that to make the week worthwhile. He decided to make an effort at conversation. Luna had gone to so much trouble for him with her movie-star routine. And he'd become nothing but grumpy. He asked, "What charity did you choose to have Madison donate to?"

She opened her mouth to answer and he immediately cut her off. Told her all about the memorial garden he'd planted for his family. "And I thought that perhaps because that was meaningful for me, it might be for a lot of people, as well. To have a perpetual garden to embody the everlasting love they feel for their departed."

"That's lovely."

He took a couple of eager bites, noticing for the first time that he was hungry.

"But then I got to thinking," he went on, "that not everyone has a piece of land that they can plant on. So I had the idea to buy small plots here and there and turn them into community memorials. Where people from a lane or village could work together, kids and seniors alike. To collectively nurture their memories."

"How thoughtful."

He forked a few more bites of succulent fish and washed them down with ice-cold beer. "I felt it would be very special to me if Madison could make her donation to the project. Even though it was my money, some of the gardens could be in her name. And since this week is meant to be a step forward for me, that would resonate and be something I'd remember."

"What a wonderful idea."

"I'm sorry," he said, realizing he hadn't let her answer. "I asked about what charity *you* were supporting and then blathered on about mine. You make me want to share every thought that comes into my mind. You have a strange effect on me, Luna Price."

CHAPTER SEVEN

CHARLIE HELD LUNA'S hand as he led her to
the ocean. It was the dark of night save for
the stars and brilliant glow of the moon. Her
feet padded through sand as she followed
him down the beach.

"It's cool," she exclaimed once her toes
made contact with the water, although it
wasn't unpleasant as the easy waves gurgled over her ankles. "Feels good."

What also felt good was him holding her
hand, and she hoped he wouldn't let go. His
profile in the night caught her eye and then
she wasn't able to tear her gaze away. Wad-
ing into the water and holding hands with
this special man was like being on another
planet, so far from the therapy sessions and
doldrums the last months in Kentucky had
become. It was time to move forward and as
a manifestation of that she stepped farther

into the water, still holding Charlie's hand as they immersed their legs up to their knees.

"The breeze across my chest with my feet in the water is a sublime combination," he remarked. "You had a good idea to come out for a night swim."

She was pleased that he was enjoying the activity. It had become obvious that Charlie was having a hard day and they'd postponed their plans to visit the city of Old San Juan until tomorrow. Luna had briefly considered booking an outing for herself and leaving him to rest and recuperate. Toying with a spa visit, another outdoor sport or maybe a shopping excursion to browse a local market, she instead decided to stay at the villa with him.

Earlier, she seemed to have had his full attention when she'd gussied up into movie-star garb and shown him a bit of how the Hollywood factory worked. It delighted her to no end that he didn't like all the fakery. She'd begun thinking that although it was nothing compared to the loss he had suffered, she'd known plenty of her own pain and that perhaps the heavens had sent Charlie to her as a balm, if not a cure. With it being her job to do the same for him.

Just like Charlie, part of Luna's objective in this M match was to broach the idea of dating again. She knew if she did, after everything she'd been through, it was not going to be the superficial, red-carpet appearance, where she was eye candy on the arm of eye candy. And she'd have to do a better job of guarding herself from piranhas like Troy Lutt, even if they were sent her way by well-meaning connections. If she was ever going to date again, other than necessary public appearances, it was going to be with someone noble. Someone like Charlie. She was so drawn to him, a man who walked with his pain in tow, who was only capable of being true to who he was. Flesh and blood. And tears.

"Let's go farther," he said as he tugged her hand and they plunged into the water up to their waists.

"Farther," she whispered to herself.

She knew that those one-time passionate kisses they'd shared had simply been on impulse—two people thrown together who had laid themselves bare to each other. But it was fleeting, and it meant nothing.

Which was fine. Better to know that right away, she thought, even as he held her hand firmly in his under the water. She didn't come to this M week with the intention of meeting her soul mate. They were here for a night swim, just to have some more relaxing entertainment, and that was it. She challenged, "Ready to go for it?"

"You mean in and under?"

"We're not just going to stay waist-deep, are we?"

"I'll go in farther if you will."

"Holding hands?"

"No, I think we'll need both our arms to swim."

He released his grip on her hand. She missed it instantly but knew it was necessary. "Let's try to stay beside each other."

"One. Two. Three. Go."

And with that, Luna swam into the ocean, allowing her head to dunk under as she stroked. The water was fairly calm so she wasn't afraid. Taking quick glances to the side, she saw Charlie's head bobbing as he swam, as well. Her heart began to pump with the exertion of swimming into the tide and she welcomed the extra oxygen intake with each breath.

When she reached the point where she couldn't dig her feet into the sand while keeping her head above water, she began to move to stay afloat. Charlie bridged the distance between them.

"The Pacific is too cold to swim in at night so this is a rare treat," she said.

"Thank you for sharing about your life in California. I can appreciate how stressful it must be, having how you look being intrinsic to your profession." He swam around her a bit.

"It's relentless. The paparazzi, or some sexist producer, is always there to mess up your confidence."

"Is it worth it?"

She snickered. "I've achieved my dreams. I've been very lucky and can't complain. But it cost me a lot, that's for sure."

"How long do you think you'll keep doing it?"

"As I'm sure you've heard, Hollywood isn't kind to women when they age. Sometimes the decision is made for you when you just don't get the roles anymore."

"What would you do instead?"

"I've always thought I might like to make smaller films about topics that are important to women. Maybe eventually as a producer."

"A glittering star with a conscience. Earlier, I'd been so busy telling you about the memorial gardens, I never got around to hearing which charity you designated for Madison's donation?"

Luna dipped her head under and whooshed up in a way that all her hair pulled backward away from her face, which made her feel clean and unfettered.

"There's a campaign that reaches out to teenagers to promote body positivity. If they need counseling and they're not able to afford it, this organization provides it."

"Ah, something very personal to you."

"Yes. I mean, I'm part of that illusion that could lead someone to feel that they don't measure up to a certain beauty standard. Heck, I feel that way every day—that I'm the one who doesn't measure up! It's very twisted."

Charlie got close. Only a few inches close, but as her hands paddled to stay afloat, her leg touched his under the water and their arms brushed by mistake. "Do you not realize how beautiful you are, Luna? Inside and out."

"Hollywood is a very complex place. There are the most wonderful, creative people there, but there are also those whose sole purpose is to bring others down."

"I hope your time away from the limelight has shown you that it's only what you think of yourself that matters."

"Honestly, I hope so, too."

"I wish you could see yourself through my eyes."

He stopped swimming. Planted his feet. The waterline hit him at chest height. Once standing tall, he reached for her and pulled her to him. He placed his hands on both sides of her waist and lifted her up so that her face met his, their lips so near they were almost touching.

And then they were.

Was Charlie dreaming? Perhaps this was a strange doze of a nap taking him in and out of consciousness, as he kissed Luna in the ocean under the moon. But as his mouth pressed incessantly against the sublime plushness that was her lips, his nerve endings couldn't lie. He was very, very awake. When he craned his head back a little bit to gaze into her twinkling eyes, he had to believe the moment was actually happening. As soon as he did, his mouth returned to hers, eager, desperate to continue what was surely the most pleasant activity he'd experienced in as long as he could remember.

Nimble hands clasped around his neck and slim forearms encircled him, making him feel part of her. Beneath the water, it was a natural next move for her legs to wrap around his waist. It had been ten years since he'd felt a woman there, not to mention with the added sensation of the warm water they were immersed in.

In what was at first instinct until it became a decision, he submerged his arms to lift her tightly against him, one hand under each of her thighs until their centers pressed into each other save for the scraps of fabric between them. His core convulsed, raging with desire. They locked against each other, the ocean's current swaying around them.

"Is this wrong, Luna?" The question popped without forethought. They'd vowed not to have physical contact again. He hadn't come to Puerto Rico for romance or sex. "I wasn't expecting to feel the way I do about you."

He didn't give her a chance to answer before he had to take her mouth again with his. Swirling into a vortex of kisses, time under the stars stood still. All he could do was explore her. The tip of his tongue met hers in a slow dance that lasted forever, their lips sealed together. Her mouth was warm inside, charging him with internal excitement. He had a moment's wonder if even the ocean wouldn't be big enough to contain the surge of longing Luna had set free in him.

And surely she didn't object to his kisses as she returned each one, seemingly with the same gusto as he was giving. She confided, "I haven't been able to relax with somebody in a long time. If ever."

Amelia, who had been in the far recesses of his mind, made her way forward. Was kissing Luna a betrayal to her memory? That question, while standing in the middle of the ocean, with Luna's long legs gripped around him, demanded to be answered. Charlie already knew what Amelia would say. What she'd been saying for years. Yet he hadn't been able to listen.

Of course, she'd want him to be with someone else. If the situation had been reversed, he'd want the same for her. It went without saying that she wouldn't approve of what he'd become—an abandoned billionaire rattling around a dusty mansion with nothing to look forward to, no one to share anything with. She wouldn't have wanted her and Lily's deaths to become his, as had been the case. With every fiber of her being she would have hoped for his contentment. That he would know trust again. Find joy. Maybe even have more children. In any case, she'd have hated him for throwing his chance at happiness away because theirs had died. He wished that Amelia would send him a direct sign that she approved of his actions. But maybe she had and he wasn't able to see it.

He slowly ran his hands up Luna's spine and her passion seized his full attention. The way her back arched in response to his touch fueled the demand in his body, too. His arousal was growing to breaking point. When his hands slid up to her shoulders, he hooked his thumbs into each of the straps of her swimsuit. He slowly inched it downward, and gasped at seeing the first swell of her breasts. She gave him a smile, so that he was assured of her approval. The sight of that intimate skin glistening wet in the moonlight caused emotion to lodge in his throat. He was a sexual being again, a man with needs and wants and the vigor to pursue them!

He tugged her swimsuit done farther. With her legs still around him for leverage, his hands cupped her firm, tender breasts. His palms made wide circles, as he wanted to cover every inch, feel every graceful curve. Could there be a piece of art that was greater perfection than the slopes of her body? He thought not. When his fingertips rolled on her nipples, her head fell back in pleasure, encouraging him to continue.

Yearning demanded more as his hands went around to support her back. He kissed the center of her throat, his mouth trailing its elegant length down into the crook of her neck, then out to her shoulders and back again. Waves lapped around him, creating a world where liquid and solid were the same. He couldn't get enough. As soon as he found himself in one spot, he longed for the next. His mouth experienced ecstasy, as he kissed, licked, bit. She held his head to her, fingers moving through his wet hair as she moaned softly.

After an eternity like that, the roused man who had spent so many years in a lifeless state wanted even more. He peeled Luna's swimsuit down even more, his hands appreciating every inch of her sleek skin.

"Luna," he whispered as he kissed her ear, "if I take your swimsuit off, we may lose it to the Caribbean. Can I order you some new ones tomorrow?"

She laughed, a dulcet tone that melded with the percussion of the mild waves. "That's okay. I brought several others."

With all the permission he needed, he pulled the suit off her. He tossed it behind him and they heard a splash, both of them giggling as the garment sailed on its merry way to fates unknown.

Charlie's entire body pulsed at the thought, and sight, of Luna now naked in his arms, under no one's eyes but the moon's.

Left. Right. Behind. Underneath. Luna couldn't take her hands off formidable Charlie. A sweep along the side of his torso, rock-solid, entranced her so she indulged in it over and over, making mental notes of each toned muscle. The arousal in his eyes told her he appreciated the sensation as much as she did. This was new to both of them, but it was as if they were kindred spirits who had known each other for a lifetime. Merely returning home. Her fingertips tingled as she ran them along his chest, not learning but instead revisiting a place she hadn't been for far too long. She couldn't fathom how she'd become so attached to Charlie in such a short time, yet she had— her own caution, his rocky moods and the emotions only adding to the bond.

He brought her to him for another prolonged kiss, the taste of the ocean bracing his lips. She wrapped herself around him again, now naked, a creature of the sea, her hair cascading behind her like a mythological mermaid. Normally, Luna would be self-conscious. The famous actress whose likeness could be found not only on the big screen, but also on billboards and city buses. The world had had opportunity to study her and her body for years, a freakish reality that most people would never experience. They had indeed examined her. And had photographed, videoed, talked about, written, posted, tweeted and by every other method commented. She had been reduced to a product they were either going to buy or not buy, and if they did, would surely leave a user review for all to see. Those glaring eyes had driven Luna into an illness she had only recently come to understand.

Yet here, with Charlie, the sea and the sky the only witnesses, she genuinely felt natural and beautiful. The water was exquisite and Charlie's height and long arms were a life raft that made her feel both liberated and shielded. Her hands continued exploring him everywhere they could reach. Until his swim trunks became an obstacle.

"Fair's fair, Charlie." She grinned. "I sacrificed a bathing suit. I think you'll have to, as well."

"Only if you can get it off me," he flirted, making her surge her with anticipation. Was this really all right? she asked herself. To have enough faith in him to not use her? This accomplished man didn't want anything from her, didn't need her for personal leverage. It was okay to just have a good time with him tonight, wasn't it? So what if soon they'd part and become nothing but each other's pleasant holiday recollection. Tomorrow's worries could wait, couldn't they?

Opening her eyes wide to his challenge, she swooped one leg and then the other away from him and thrust her hands underwater. Trying to find a hold to yank on his trunks, she bobbed so much in the water that he broke away. And chuckled.

"You're. Laughing. At. Me?"

"I told you, you have to pull them off." He lifted his arms as if to make it easier for her, but when she was able to latch on to the fabric again, he managed to twist away. "Come get me, movie star."

She scrunched her nose in pretend frustration. "I'm after you, CEO." And, with that, Luna lunged at him. He broke loose again, but not before she managed to get a good hold on the elastic waistband against the small of his back. He tried to swim away, but this time the trunks didn't go with him. A jerk on her side, a twirl on his and, finally, triumph was hers. She held the suit high in one hand like a victory flag and then flung it adrift. Both of them exploded into laughter.

He brought her to him. There was nothing funny about the smoothness of his hips, which she could now splay her hands against, without barrier. And then to his sturdy haunches. His arousal pressed against her and she reached for it, velvety in the water but rigid and throbbing underneath the skin. She stroked in a manner that must have been pleasurable to him because he shut his eyes. His face was magnificent in the night. The straight nose and long eyelashes. Shadows accentuated his prominent jaw, which she kissed her way along, still maneuvering her hand under the water. Her mouth rode leisurely down the center of his chest, the wet skin somehow tasting like sunshine. Her titillation grew to an unexpected urgency.

"Let's go," she said, just as she did *let go* of him, which produced just the result she was after: an agonized moan from his sexy mouth.

"Argh, what are you doing to me?"

"Race you to shore." She didn't wait for a response and boldly took off with confident strokes. He followed.

When they reached the dry land in front of their villa, Luna quickly said, "I'll be right back." She dashed into the master bathroom, where she'd seen condoms in the lavish basket of toiletries provided. Grabbing them with a salacious smile no one saw, she rushed back out. Only to be immediately tackled by Charlie, who pulled her down atop the towels he'd laid out on the beach.

The sand was easy under her back as Charlie caressed both of her arms, from her shoulders all the way down to her fingertips. He came back via her torso, slowly up her rib cage. She had a moment's wince of insecurity about her body. Eating disorders could bring confusion. Sometimes she thought she was too thin, other times overweight. On hiatus from everything including men, part of her therapy was to reckon with herself as a sexual being, as desirable, regardless of what her disease was telling her.

Charlie wasn't judging her. Measuring her. Calculating how to take advantage of her. His moves were an expression of pure truth, of male hunger, of a need they both had. She knew she was strong enough now to quell those voices in her head that caused her to doubt her beauty.

Remembering one of the mantras learned in therapy, she chanted it inside her head. *You are perfect just as you are.*

As the late-night winds wisped over her naked body, his mouth covered hers…until it started to travel once again. The inside of her wrist. The side of her leg. He kissed her breasts. Her stomach. Anywhere he went, she welcomed it. He lifted his head and whispered, "You are more luminous than the Caribbean moon that watches over us."

"You're beautiful, too, Charlie."

With that, he put on the condom and moved back up so that he could kiss her mouth as their bodies joined completely, undulating together in the sand, mimicking the perfect rhythm of the tide's ebb and flow.

CHAPTER EIGHT

"'THE COLONIAL ARCHITECTURE is indicative of the Spanish influence in Puerto Rico,'" Luna said, reading from the touring app she'd downloaded to her phone as she and Charlie roamed the picturesque city streets. "*Viejo*—that means old. San Juan is known for its colorful buildings and cobblestone streets."

"Does it say anything about why the cobblestones are blue?"

"They're called *adoquines*, and they're a waste product of iron smelting that was brought from Spain."

The sky was unclouded, the air was clean and Luna Price was the most enchanting being in the universe. In her cotton coral-colored dress and flat brown sandals, she looked like a carefree tourist, blending right in, not attracting notice except perhaps for her simple loveliness. That Charlie had just spent a mind-altering night of lovemaking with a famous actress, no less, seemed utterly surreal in the noonday sun.

"Shall we look in that shop?" he asked as he presented his arm to help her navigate across the stones and their uneven surface. A bell attached to the front door chimed when they entered.

"Pretty," Luna said as she admired the jewelry on display. "I saw a description on the app. These are Taino pieces, the jewelry of the native people in Puerto Rico."

"Te gusta?" asked the shopkeeper, an older woman with a friendly grin.

"*Si.* Very unique. What are they made from?"

"Clay, wood and leather."

"I like those earrings." She gestured to a pair that were long and dangly, with beads that seemed to be made out of dried clay.

"Each has a sun pendant on the bottom," the woman pointed out.

"Hold them up to your face," Charlie suggested. The shopkeeper handed Luna a mirror. She brought one of the earrings to her delicate lobe. Charlie was struck with the impulse to take said earlobe between his teeth as he had last night, but he knew this was not the time or place. In fact, it would be smart if he never took Luna's earlobe, or any other part of her, into his mouth ever again. Although that sounded to him like an unimaginable fate.

Oh, how luscious last night had been, the feeling of his bareness in the sea, an organism in the biotic world, in the wild. And, to boot, in the company of the most vital and sensual woman he had ever known. Together they had intermingled in an aquatic dance of kisses and limbs. Then they took their voyage to shore, to the tender sands where they brought each other to ecstasy again and again as the waves provided music for their journey.

But where was he now? Charlie tried to understand as he watched Luna admire the jewelry. He hadn't agreed to the M Agency agreement for this, to be totally entranced by a woman who had come here to help with her rehabilitation, just as he had. He wasn't ready for the *real thing* with anyone…was he?

"May I buy those for you, Luna?"

She giggled a bit before answering. "I have my own money, you know." Which actually was funny, as she possessed, no doubt, a substantial fortune.

"I know, but it would mean a lot to me to give them to you." Words were falling out of his mouth with him not even sure where they were coming from. But he did want to buy the earrings.

"That would be very kind, Charlie. Thank you."

Outside of the shop, Luna took the earrings from the tissue they'd been wrapped in. "I think I'd like to wear these today. Can you help me put them on?"

Eager, he held the delicacy of Luna's ear in what felt like the most important job in the world. The earrings looked perfect with her outfit as they resumed their touring.

They visited Viejo San Juan's best-known landmark. El Morro or, properly, Castillo San Felipe del Morro, the fortress and military outpost. Construction on the massive structure began in 1539 by Spanish settlers and it was in use until 1961, when the US Army retired it to establish a museum. They walked through the recreations of the barracks and kitchens, which showed how the soldiers there might have lived. From the outdoor top levels, they could see the Atlantic Ocean. Charlie's gut panged when he envisioned a few days from now, when the week would end and he'd depart for the UK, and she would go in the opposite direction, to LA. The distances of land and sea had never seemed greater to him.

He surprised himself with the thought that Luna mattered to him now, something he'd never have imagined when he'd first arrived in Puerto Rico. They strolled the vast front lawn of the fortress. He blinked twice to make sure he was seeing clearly and not hallucinating. Dozens of people were flying colorful kites.

"It's a local tradition to fly kites on this lawn, according to my travel guide," Luna said, reading from her app. The kites sailed through the air, held aloft by everyone from squealing schoolchildren to seniors to tour groups in matching T-shirts. "Is something wrong?"

He hadn't realized that his emotions had registered on his face. His Amelia had loved kite flying. He could remember many occasions, now parading through his mind, when the weather was optimal and she'd drag him along with her to do so. Selecting one of the half-dozen kites she owned, she'd pile a pic-

nic basket into the car and off they'd go. He
always enjoyed himself so much because of
her enjoyment of the activity.

"I can't wait until we share this pleasure
with our children," she'd said one happy day
early in her pregnancy, smiling and caress-
ing her burgeoning baby bump, her kite
high. Charlie's throat tightened as he kept
his now glassy eyes fixed on the vibrant
display, unable to articulate the aching in
his chest.

But afterward, sitting on a bench in one
of the charming town squares of Viejo San
Juan, his temperament lightened. His outstretched arm made its way around Luna's
shoulder and they sat watching the pedes-
trians promenade this way and that. She
hadn't pursued an explanation as to what
had bothered him while watching the kites
fly. He sensed she knew that in that moment he was being torn down by the past.
It was as if she understood. His ease around
her was presenting a new world. One that
was confusing. One that he certainly didn't
have a map for.

"Shall we eat?" he suggested after noticing that the sun was moving. It was important for Luna to eat at consistent intervals.

"I found a recommendation from the resort's list."

They turned onto a street with the most vividly painted buildings Charlie had ever seen. From mint-green to petal-pink to lavender to pale yellow, with all of the windowsills and trim done in white. Wrought-iron balconies displayed flower boxes. The café had a patio shaded by red umbrellas. He pulled out a white chair for Luna to sit in, then positioned his next to hers rather than across. That way he could be next to her and they could both gaze out to the narrow lane.

"Everything looks good," Luna said as she perused the menu. "I've read the starter dish of sweet eggplant is really special."

"And for the main course, let's try the steak Fortaleza."

"Which means fort."

"Beer to drink."

When the waiter arrived, Charlie ordered, pleased with his pronunciations.

"Thank you again for these," she said as she fingered an earring. They had been priced comparably to the beer he'd just ordered, yet he felt on top of the world that she liked them. He had to remind himself that he was the CEO of a billion-pound corporation. Not a barefoot boy infatuated with a pretty girl on a sunny island.

The food was delectable. The grilled eggplant drizzled with locally produced honey tasted like gold. The steak was sliced open and stuffed inside with ham, cheese, onions and peppers, and served with a creamy mushroom sauce on top. It was exquisite. As was his companion.

"Buena noches," the catamaran driver welcomed Charlie and Luna as they boarded for their short cruise to Vieques Island after they'd eaten.

"Buena noches." Luna greeted the middle-aged man with bulky muscles straining against his white T-shirt and shorts.

"Have you been enjoying your stay in Puerto Rico?"

"Si, the food is delicious and today we toured the city."

"You are in for a very special night."

As they left shore, the speed at which they channeled through the water had the wind whipping through Luna's hair and against her skin. It felt extreme and adventurous. As it did having Charlie beside her. He had made such impassioned love to her the night before it still reverberated through her. Yes, he was a man who had endured the most unspeakable agonies, which still overtook him and attacked without warning—as she'd witnessed this afternoon, under the pleasant skies as the two of them had watched the kite flyers—but perhaps because of his pain, rather than in spite of it, the fervor that they shared in the sand last night had shot to her core. He was a realist, he didn't pretend like everything was perfect, didn't live in fantasyland. Popularity and approval had no meaning to him. She respected him. And he had made her start to believe in something that she'd never dared to before.

As they arrived on the small island, she looked forward to seeing a famed Puerto Rican attraction, the brightest biolumines-cent bay in the world. At the shoreline, the kayaks and wet suits they'd reserved were waiting. Once ready, under the starry sky, they paddled with oars into the center of Mosquito Bay. Like many visitors to Puerto Rico, they'd come to see one of nature's most unusual displays. Millions, maybe bil-lions, of tiny microorganisms lived in the water of the bay. And when the water was disturbed by the oars of a kayak, or even by a hand through the waves, the organisms lit up, creating a light show. It was an environmental phenomenon, and the sheer brilliance was hard to believe. Luna gasped at the sight.

"How stunning," Charlie called out, turning back toward Luna from his position in the front of the kayak. With other people in kayaks or boats all around them, the explosions of light came from every direction, radiant bright blue erupting from the still black water.

"How can this be?"

"The natural world is humbling."

Temporarily holding his oar in only one hand, Charlie reached his other hand behind him to grab hold of one of Luna's so that they could be joined while experiencing this marvel. After they took it all in for a few minutes, he lowered their clasped hands into the water beside the kayak and splashed, so that they could provoke the light with their own hands. They sprayed light toward each other, laughing at the miracle of it.

Oh, Charlie, she thought. How was she ever going to forget this week? To move on as planned, and go back to California and the pressures that had done so much damage to her? She'd been unprofessional in her exit a year ago. Desperate, she'd left that set even though production had almost begun. She'd inconvenienced the rest of the cast, the crew, her agent and all of her team, and cost the studio a lot of money. Even if the year she'd spent in recovery made her question whether she still wanted to stay within the Hollywood machine anymore, she had to at least return to make good on the contract she'd signed. The dreams she'd sometimes had about making her own movies, expressing her art in way that she was in control of, seemed out of reach until she cleaned up the mess she'd left. Maybe she was ready to leave the industry entirely. Go back to Kentucky, perhaps? Help her parents with the ranch as they grew older? Invest in a business? Whatever the case, she had to return to LA first and see everything through.

As planned, she'd leave Dorada and all that had happened there behind. Leave Charlie behind. A man who she was beginning to think she might like to stay near, and not just in Puerto Rico… In his own awkward way he'd made her feel completely accepted. Made her imagine a lifestyle she had never dared to consider.

Last night, after they'd brought each other pleasure upon pleasure with their bodies and, she had to admit, their souls, they'd stretched out in the sand and looked up to the sky. He'd reached for a beach blanket to cover them and they rested, spent and hazy. She got lost in thought about different roads her life could have taken and sensed Charlie's mind had gone to a similar place. It was comfortable to be beside him.

After a while, though, it had gotten cold, and she was sleepy so they went back into the villa. She hoped he'd join her in the bedroom, where they could sleep in a lover's embrace. But he'd said he wasn't tired and wanted to check on some work. They shared a sensuous kiss good-night, yet she retreated to the master suite alone with a ring of sadness through her bones.

In the center of the plush bed, surrounded by pillows and bedding, she'd convinced herself it was for the best. Someone who pretended for a living should surely know not to get sucked into the charade. This week with Charlie was simply what it was intended to be. Thinking of it otherwise could only lead to disappointment and pain. Even if she was willing to reconsider her own oath, his was to never love a woman again. She doubted he'd go back on his word to the memory of his family.

"That was just extraordinary," Charlie said when they got back to the villa after the bioluminescent bay. "I think I'd like to return to Puerto Rico someday."

"Soon it will be time to go home."

"For you, the word *home* must have two separate meanings."

"Home is Los Angeles," she affirmed. "I really do have a gorgeous house in the hills. Panoramic views, lots of light. I'm very fortunate."

"Why doesn't that sound convincing?"

"I'm apprehensive about going back. I hope I'm strong enough for all of it this time."

"It seems like you'll be returning with your eyes wide open."

He made her feel so reassured. What would it be like to have someone on her side, by her side, all the time? While her team was loyal, she'd never let anyone in that close. She'd never dared because there had never been anyone who wasn't affiliated with Luna Price, the commodity, rather than just plain Luna Price, the woman. That she'd begun to think Charlie was that one elusive person—the exception to the rule—was a hazardous game. Even if she was ready to let someone in, Charlie wore his tragedy as a barrier. He wasn't going to let go of what had come to define him. And he was entitled to that, if that was what he wanted.

But tonight was different than last night's parting. Tonight it came as a shock when they were standing between the living room and the bedroom and he backed Luna against the doorway and pressed himself into her. Trapping her with an arm on either side of her head, he kissed her with a verve that made her knees tremble. Forcing his whole body against hers, she felt his arousal in full strength. He ground into her with force. "Luna," he rasped in her ear. "Luna."

The unadulterated eroticism ran purple through her veins. To be so desired stirred her profoundly and her body yielded to his. Their lips met, tongues desperate for more. Then, all at once, he lifted her into his arms and carried her to the previously unchartered kingdom of the master bed.

When Charlie felt the glow of sunlight on his eyelids, they clicked open. His surroundings were strange. He'd become accustomed to the grooves of the sofa cushions, where he'd been laying his bones at night, and the play of light and shadow from that vantage point. He knew he was still in the villa, with the wafting scent of the courtyard flowers and the sounds of morning waves just steps away. The silky warmth next to him made his head turn in that direction. Luna, curled toward him, eyes closed, was a sight to behold.

He realized that of all the extraordinary things that had taken place since he'd come to Puerto Rico, what happened last night beat them all. Not the surreal show of nature's lights on Vieques Island. Not even the sizzling lovemaking that he and Luna had engaged in. No, the most surprising turn of events was that Charlie had slept. Slept! All night!

He'd forgotten what a rested body felt like. With each breath, oxygen traveled to the far reaches of his bloodstream, which hadn't received any in a decade. The pervasive tightness across his forehead was gone. The little niggles of aches that he'd sometimes spent the night distracted by were imperceptible.

His muscles were relaxed but invigorated. His mouth ticked up in approval.

"Good morning," Luna cooed as her eyes opened and she stretched her arms above her head.

A quick check of Charlie's phone confirmed what he'd already suspected. "*Buenas tardes.* It's afternoon already." Yes, he'd slept not just through the dark hours, but well past the first light of dawn.

"Hmmm," she sang, a tiny murmur that reminded him of some of the sounds of pleasure that had come from her throat last night. Sounds he most definitely wouldn't mind hearing more of.

He brushed away errant golden strands in front of her face and his fingers lingered in her luxurious hair, intertwining the locks in his fingers. It was something he thought could occupy him for hours. "What do you want to do today?"

"According to our itinerary, tonight we're going to a rum tasting. And to hear live music and have dancing lessons."

"Dancing lessons?"

"Yes. Apparently we both told Madison that we enjoyed music so she's set up an evening where we're going to learn the traditional bomba style of Puerto Rican dance."

His brow crinkled. "I don't know about that." Although really, why not? What did he have to lose? Charlie Matthews was finally aroused and flourishing again. What would be better than dancing the night away with this amazing creature on their island paradise?

"So how shall we spend a few hours until then?" she asked.

Instead of answering, he showed her. With every fiber in his being.

As the sun moved through the afternoon, they laid with their limbs in a tangle after having brought each other to bliss once again. He wheeled the food cart into the bedroom and fed her a meaty grilled sandwich and juicy fruits. They lolled in a half daze for who knew how long, adjusting now and then to reach for a different part of each other. Something that he was certain he could happily do for an endless amount of time.

Endless. His own words repeated over and over and over in his head. He thought of yesterday. Of visiting the fort and how seeing those kites in the sky had reminded him that he'd never be granted for a second time the conjugal peace and security that he had with Amelia. That had been a once-in-a-lifetime love, snatched from him along with the expression of that love, their baby girl, her sweet orange ringlet curls like those of her pretty mother's.

The kites at the fort were little demons in the sky, sent in a swarm to encircle and torment him lest he begin to have too much sincere companionship and enjoyment with this new woman, who had brought optimism back to a heart that had decided against it. Lest he feel slightly less alone and lonely. That was how his life had worked since Amelia and Lily died and he assumed it would always be that way. The gravity of the universe saw to it that Charlie stayed casting downward. And if, even for a second, his neck tilted backward so that his eyes could look ahead, forces knocked him to the ground. Showed him a sign.

Wait a minute. A sign! Hadn't he begged Amelia to send him a signal? Did the holy spirit, the ancient qi, the essence of his young wife that stayed tucked inside him, communicate as he'd begged her to? To let him know that she wished for him to be complete again, to inhale with all of the power in his lungs. To smile and laugh and stumble and share his days and nights with another woman. He'd directly asked Amelia if it was okay to love again.

Was her vibration within him calling out to be heard? Had it actually been her handiwork that Charlie had taken this trip to Puerto Rico? Did Amelia put Luna in his path because she'd chosen her for him? And decided that they would visit that fort to make him see that there were still blue skies and August breezes to be had? And that, yes, she wanted him to find delight and fulfillment with someone new?

CHAPTER NINE

"Salud!" Charlie tipped his rum glass to touch Luna's and then they both sipped.

"This is the amber?" With six glasses in front of them, each with a small pour of translucent liquid of varying hues, she wanted to make sure.

"Yes, that one is considered to have a rich, full body."

Luna knew to only take small sips of the offering as she didn't want to become sleepy. They still had plans to go dancing, which she was greatly looking forward to.

He read aloud from the laminated card that had arrived with their tasting flight in the secluded high-backed booth at the dark bar. "There are eighty types of rum. And it's Puerto Rico's chief export. It's been produced here since the fifteenth century as a by-product of the sugarcane industry."

"Its base is molasses, right?"

"Yes, it's then mixed with water and fermented." As they talked, Charlie ran his finger under the thin strap of the red tank top Luna wore. Uncharacteristically for her, she was baring a lot of skin in the wisp of a covering that seemed right for working up a sweat on a hot summer night. Although he needed to behave himself with that delicate tug on the thin fabric's strap, she mused, because his touch was so distracting she might forget about the dancing plan after all.

"The darker varieties are aged in charred barrels. That's why they have a stronger flavor." He teased her by continuing to both lightly tap his fingers on her shoulder and read from the information card.

"Let's try the one called silver."

He picked up the glass of one of the clear tastes and brought it to her lips. She sipped and then he made sure to bring his mouth to the exact spot where hers had touched the glass to take his own sip, the move not lost on her. "That one is so much lighter. It would be nice in a mixed cocktail."

"Mmm," he answered, but seemed more focused on running one finger up and over that strap of her top and into the crook of her neck, a sensation so exquisite it made her back arch.

As suggested, she'd dressed traditionally for their bomba lesson later. The Dorada staff had provided her with a long skirt of many ruffles and a tremendous amount of volume, the type that would open to a full circle if laid on the ground. The outer fabric was white with beautifully applied red fabric flowers. And the underside of the skirt was a dense floral pattern of many colors. When she danced, she would lift them up with her hands, so the detail was important to both sides of the construction of the skirt. Included in her delivery to the villa was one perfect hibiscus, the national flower, along with hairpins for her to wear it behind one ear. Choosing her own red tank top to match, the outfit gave her a sexy, potent feel.

Charlie wore his own white jeans and untucked white shirt, the color men typically dressed in for the dance. His eyes were like iridescent emeralds, and she tingled at the memories of his commanding mouth covering every inch of her during the lazy sensual afternoon they'd spent in bed.

"Now the spiced rum." She lifted a taste of another one.

"Golden color with spices and caramel sometimes added."

"Yes, I taste that." It was the flavor of him she was tasting, though. He pervaded all of her senses and she could only drink, hear and breathe him. Her thoughts shocked her. She'd assumed, accepted even, that a true and meaningful relationship wasn't on her horizon, especially after years of being taken advantage of and basically used as a human ladder for other people's ascension. She'd considered that weasel Troy Lutt the last time she'd even try. Maybe she could find some decent guys, not in the entertainment industry, to occasionally date. That would have to be enough.

When they got to the dance club, it was as lively and invigorating a scene as the mind could imagine. People were dancing both inside and outside on the patio, which gave way to a public plaza, and all the way around the fountain that anchored the cobblestone space. At the designated spot, they met up with the teacher, named Julia, and the small group of other students. Dressed in a purple-and-yellow dancing costume, Julia gave them a brief background on the cultural traditions. "Bomba is both the dance and the name of the musical instruments," she said while pointing to a row of seated men, each with drums that they beat in steady rhythms. "It originates from the heritage of the African slaves who were brought here to work on the sugar plantations. It is not just a dance, it is a part of our culture."

Luna's hips were already beginning to sway to the seductive percussion. She followed as Julia instructed the women to lift their skirts and to swish and sway them in aggressive expressions and with passion. She continued, "Tell a story with your skirts and your movements. The dancer leads the music rather than the other way around."

Charlie moved to the tempo, as well, although seemed unsure of what to do quite yet. He smiled watching Luna take to the dance and wave her skirt to and fro while shimmying her shoulders.

"Senors," Julia called out to the gentlemen, "you make strong, jerky and sudden movements that originate in your belly." At first, Charlie followed the moves of some of the experienced men in the crowd with a little inhibition, but then he started to move more assuredly. He gyrated, letting the dance emerge from him organically. The grind of his hips made Luna forget how to swallow air.

Together, they abandoned themselves to the rhythm, to the plaza full of people, all engrossed in a near-spiritual experience as they danced and danced and danced. All grooving together, locals and tourists, young and old, faces of every creed and color, the drumbeats taking them higher and higher. People smiled at each other. Flirted. Watched the children with delight. There was one pronounced feeling that swept through the air so distinctly you could almost see it. Love.

As the beats mesmerized their minds while their bodies moved with openness, it was a moment of profound connectedness to everything around her that Luna had never felt before. That reassured her she was finally mentally and physically on a healthy road after a dark year. The past hadn't defeated her. In fact, she was mighty. Luna Price was back. Because of the bomba. Because of the skirt she wore that encouraged her to write her own narrative, and be nothing more or less than who she was. Because of the balmy winds of Puerto Rico, which she would never forget. But most of all because of this unforgettable man in white dancing in front of her. A man to whom she didn't know how she was going to bid adios.

The next day, as Charlie reached down for Luna's hand to help pull her up a steep incline, he thought about how Puerto Rico had seeped into his bloodstream. Today, deep into the misty El Yunque rain forest, the scent was so fresh he wished never to smell anything else. Countless species of plant life surrounded them and only the rustle of nature filled their ears. He pointed to a flock of birds. "Look at them."

Soaring, the winged creatures were the embodiment of liberty. He wished he could somehow join them, taking Luna along, of course. But the end was near, and they would not fly away together. Charlie was to return home tomorrow to England, to his artifact of a mansion. A changed man, just as was the plan, but the gains somehow seemed hollow in the face of having to part from Luna.

After a long hike in which they saw wildlife, including the famous coqui frogs, which were endemic to Puerto Rico, they visited the Yokahú observation tower, with its stunning views of the vast green mountains and the ocean.

"It's been an amazing week here, hasn't it?" he said from the top of the tower, where they were standing, holding hands, taking it all in.

"I can't believe it's coming to an end."

"What if we didn't leave just yet?" he offered, slightly less than halfway serious. "Just because we agreed to a week with the M Dating Agency doesn't mean we have to vacate. I'll just book us in for another week." He hardly recognized his own voice but the thought of letting Luna go tomorrow was too much to endure. Last night, when they had danced with reckless abandon among the crowd in Viejo San Juan, Charlie had been ready to pull up roots and buy them a villa here that they could call their own forever.

"That's a lovely thought," Luna said with a squeeze to his hand. "In fact, you even suggesting it touches my heart." He still didn't know if he was talking realistically, but with her, he had come to start thinking out loud. "But I have to get back to LA. I really screwed up there. I have to make this film. Set wrongs to right."

Of course. Thank goodness she was the voice of reason. He was surprised he'd even had that idea. It had been crystal clear that he'd come to Puerto Rico only so that he could return to the living a little. Mission accomplished. The cobwebs had been dusted off. He was energized. But there was no point in prolonging the inevitable. His life wasn't here. Or with Luna…despite what Amelia's voice was telling him. This time, he might know better than her what he was, and wasn't, capable of.

Maybe life wasn't in the stuffy manor of Buckinghamshire anymore, either. Maybe it was time to sell that stone reminder of death, that gigantic gravestone that he had been taking cover behind. Should he buy a deluxe flat in London with all the cutting-edge bells and whistles befitting a tech billionaire? Where he could bring home beautiful women at night that he'd usher straight out the door in the morning? One thing was certain. This week had changed him forever.

He and Luna took lots of photos and selfies from the observation tower that he knew he'd look at and cherish for the rest of his life. Once back down to the ground, they were hot and sweaty, so they located one of the natural pools that El Yunque was known for. Prepared, with swimsuits under their clothes, they tossed their outer layers and jumped in. They swam to a waterfall, its rush producing a powerful roar. Charlie pulled Luna to him and wrapped first one, then the other, of her arms around his neck. His circled her waist.

"Let's come back some day." He didn't phrase it as a question.

"Yes."

"Yes."

He brought his lips to hers and kissed her as the waterfall gushed down on them. His eyes closed—he was lost in the moment. Another freeze frame that he would have and hold until his dying day. Because he didn't believe they would ever really return to the paradise of this week. That wasn't what was meant to be.

"Charlie. I have another idea," she said after an urgent round of kisses. "What if you came to LA with me? I'll be on set during the day but you could sightsee or work. We could be together in the evenings."

Go to California with her? "I can't do that."

"I know. It was just a fleeting thought," she said hastily and then took his face in her hands and kissed him again, although this time it felt a bit like goodbye.

Much as he could envision spending every day with Luna, whether ordinary or eventful, that wasn't their destiny. They both got what they'd come to Puerto Rico for. Now their kites were meant to fly off in different directions.

"Have you had breakfast?" Charlie asked as he entered the master suite, where Luna had all of her belongings and open suitcases laid out on the bed. Where last night they'd shared their bodies with each another one last time. There had been a different mood in the air, though. No longer was it a lair filled with sensuality and courage and exploration and candor. Last night the structure housed one long nonverbal farewell followed by a brief sleep. Everything that had been discovered, unleashed and enacted this week would be packed up in separate luggage and flown to separate destinations, never to comingle again.

Luna had been holding the tears back in

her eyes ever since they had woken up and Charlie excused himself to the living room, where the closet and armoire there had been his base camp, as was originally agreed upon, until the week had taken such an unlikely turn. And now the tide had reversed again, returning the universe to the configuration that was originally intended. Melancholy shaded Luna, darkening a morning that could have been cheerful in another circumstance.

"No, did you wheel the cart in?" Luna answered his inquiry without looking up. She made busywork of folding her bathing suits into a neat pile. Her vocal cords wanted to sing out for the red swimsuit lost to the Caribbean during their first glorious joining, which now felt like a lifetime ago. Since then their bodies and souls had come together so many times that the state of being apart had become the more unnatural one. She'd been reflecting on how much she'd miss him when he'd merely gone into the other room to pack. She had no idea how she was going to weather being separated by continents.

"Yes, it's in the kitchen."

"Thanks, I'll get something in a minute."

Luna would need to grab a plate to munch from while she arranged her carry-on bag. She couldn't possibly sit down opposite Charlie's eyes and exchange pleasantries about their stay at the resort. In fact, she'd be lucky if she could bundle up the pieces of her heart that had already broken off before they shattered into a million grains and scattered onto the warm sand that grounded their villa. This week had meant more to her than she could ever put into language, and she had the sense that any more said was only going to make the inevitable moment even worse.

With her back still to him as she wound the charging cords for her electronics into manageable spirals, she heard him begin talking. "Well, it's official. I haven't a thing to wear. I read we'll be having a heat spell, even hotter than here, so you'll need to take me shopping for desert-weight clothes."

The collection of words that came out of his mouth dispersed from each other and floated in space, trying to rearrange themselves into a comprehensible sentence. But Luna wasn't able to grasp hold of them. She rotated her head around, although only slightly, as she didn't feel strong enough to meet his handsome visage. "Sorry?"

"I've got the beachwear my housekeeper bought me for this trip, and a couple of English woolen suits. I don't think that'll be quite right for the west coast, will it?"

"Wha…at?" Again, Luna admonished herself not to draw any conclusions from the reference to the word *west*. Mustering courage from the tips of her toes, hoisting it up through her hips, chest and, finally, her head, she slowly turned all the way around.

There was no way she could have known about the wide grin that had been waiting for her to pivot.

"I may be a little slow on the uptake but I'm surely not a fool," he said as he stepped toward her. "Which is what I'd be if I let you fly out of my life."

"You mean…"

"Los Angeles, here we come." He closed the distance between them. He kissed her forehead, her eyebrows, cheeks, lips and chin. The breath in her chest pumped through her so fast she thought she could hear it. Not having let in just how much it was destroying her to have to part with him, the reversal switched on an adrenaline release. She felt like jumping up and down.

"What? You changed your mind? When did this happen?" she asked, throwing her arms around him with a force that bent him to the side. His chuckle against her face was delightful. "Last night, we fell asleep in each other's arms, knowing it would be our final night together."

"You'd fallen asleep, Luna. I didn't sleep a wink. I couldn't bear to miss even a second of being able to hold you."

A gulp trickled in her throat. "Charlie."

"I don't know what I'm doing. I've only known my life with Amelia and my life without her yet still tethered to her. I'm terrified but I'm willing to try, if you are."

"I am, too." Still, joy was sparking out of her. No matter what happened, at least it didn't have to end here and now. He was right—what did they possibly have to lose?

Although it was that sobering thought that robbed the smile from her face. Because there would be a lot at stake if they tried to turn this week into something more than a gateway to greener pastures, and then failed. He couldn't take any more loss, and could she withstand the disappointment? What did she know about trustworthy relationships? They both had so much to learn. Perhaps it wasn't a good idea for him to come to LA, where all her terrors lived, waiting to attack her in the night. Maybe she'd be best to return alone, to tackle those old foes first.

But looking into his eyes, it seemed anything would be worth it not to have to leave him. She deserved companionship that made her feel good inside. Without having to actively do anything but be by her side, perhaps Charlie would be a buffer between her and the jackals determined to bring her down, as per their manifesto. And he wasn't talking about relocating to California, was he? It was too early for a decision like that.

"I don't know how long I can stay," he said, beginning to provide answers to the inquiries marching across her mind like a strip of ticker tape. "As you know, I have in-person business in London I have to start attending to. But I can extend my leave for a bit. As a matter of fact, I have offices in Silicon Valley that I haven't visited for years. It would be beneficial for me to pay a visit. See people face-to-face." The high-tech bastion of Silicon Valley was just a short hour-long plane trip north from LA.

"So while I was sound asleep last night, you were concocting this whole plan?"

"That and more. I texted with an assistant to arrange for my private jet to take us to LA." She loved that he'd drafted everything out, thought to tease and tickle her with his change of plans.

After they'd packed and double-checked that they hadn't accidentally left anything behind, Luna sensed that Charlie was having the same thoughts as she was, as they took one last look throughout the villa. The secluded courtyard where they'd shared meals and secrets. The swimming pool where moods had been processed, fears laid wide. The ocean beyond where they'd played in the water and first merged bodies in the unplanned union they'd found with each other. Inside, the living room where Charlie kept his distance until there was no longer need for that. And the master bed where they'd shown each other beauty that surpassed the bright flowers and pink sunrises they'd witnessed. La Villa de Felicidad. Where two lonely souls met and had been changed for all of eternity.

"Ready?" Charlie asked and reached for her hand, the multiple meanings of his one-word question gonging through her head.

CHAPTER TEN

LUNA WAS NERVOUS while she watched her idyllic week in Puerto Rico get further and further from view as Charlie's jet soared them high into the sky. She was elated to have him unexpectedly beside her, but not knowing what the future would bring for them worried her. And she had a lot to face when she got back to LA. A year away was a very long time. But a sense of fun won over her busy mind as they chatted during the flight. "Is there anything you haven't done in LA that you'd like to?" she asked, momentarily forgetting that there were few places she could go without being recognized. While she'd been able to hide under sundresses and dark glasses in Viejo San Juan, the paparazzi in Tinseltown had a way of finding anyone and everyone, regardless of how hard they tried to be avoided.

"I've been to Los Angeles many times but I've never visited those really touristy places, like the stars on the sidewalk of Hollywood Boulevard."

"The Walk of Fame. That's a funny thing to think about seeing with me since one of those stars is mine!" She remembered the dress-up game she'd played for him at the beginning of the week, showing him how she could slide in and out of her movie-star persona. Would she be able to slip it on and off so easily once she got back to the town that only saw one of her dimensions?

"I want to see it. Will you take a photo of me with your star?"

They chuckled. Surely no one would identify her gawking at her own star, especially if she went far in the other direction by wearing baggy clothes and one of the wigs she kept at home for just such an occasion. She thought of Anush, who was on her way back to LA, as well. She'd texted with her a few times from Puerto Rico but hadn't shared any details about Charlie because none of it seemed real. It was Anush who had taught Luna how to disguise herself so that she could go out in public, as long as she was careful not to look anyone in the eye or linger anywhere too long, as the paparazzi always seemed to spot her if she wasn't ultracareful. She hoped the brutality of Los Angeles, *her* Los Angeles, wouldn't be unbearable to Charlie.

As they landed at LAX, he'd taken it upon himself to book a limo. He wouldn't have known that she usually traveled back and forth from the airport in a smaller town car. The driver of the stretch limo had to take extra caution to navigate the winding canyon roads that led to Luna's house in the hills. The white wooden security gates swung open only after Luna punched an access code into her phone.

"Luna, this is marvelous," Charlie said upon first glance of her sprawling home. She'd flown back a couple of times during her treatment in Kentucky, but she really hadn't lived here for the better part of a year. A mixture of emotions ratcheted through her—she was glad to be back but somehow dreaded it at the same time. The limo driver unloaded their bags. With more key codes, she opened the main door.

"Let me show you around." She gestured for him to follow her into the living room with its overstuffed furniture and wide-open space. Windows everywhere showcased views of LA, from the skyscrapers of downtown to the east, to the Pacific Ocean to the west.

"I don't suppose it's too difficult to wake up to a sight like that."

"I've been very fortunate."

Luna's mind spun. She was showing herself the house as much as she was to Charlie. Her home, if LA even was home anymore. It was hard to take in at the moment. The quiet day-to-day of Kentucky, with its big sky, under which she'd uncovered, aired and then stomped out a terrible chapter of her life. Then there was tropical Puerto Rico with the spicy food, spicy music and this man who'd somehow landed in the living room of what was either her palace or her prison.

Charlie was in tow for the moment, but she knew better than to believe anything permanent would grow between them. He'd clearly said as much. His unexpected presence in her life had clearly been sent to her from the gods to be the final component of her transition and healing. Which she was certainly grateful for and she needed to keep a firm hold on that outlook. On top of the strangeness of being back in the house and with Charlie, far from their secret island bliss, was the fact that she was due on set tomorrow after her long absence.

She knew what to expect. There'd be staring and assessing and gossiping. She didn't particularly like the director of this film, finding him arrogant and sexist in the tele-meetings they'd had. Not to mention that she was bored with the big films she was cast in, always as the love interest or sidekick to a man, and never a powerful woman. *Too fragile-looking.* That had been the latest explanation a casting director had given when she'd missed out on a role she'd wanted. *You could blow her over with a slight breeze.* Luna knew that wasn't who she was. But she also knew that filmmaking relied on archetypes and her place in the mythology wasn't going to change. That's why she'd thought about making her own movies, telling her own stories. But after a year away from this industry town, she had to play by the rules first, step back into the high-heeled stilettos she used to wear.

"What a kitchen," Charlie remarked, entering the large red, white and chrome room.

Memories twisted in Luna's gut, though, as they stood in the center of the open-plan layout. Because when her eating disorder had held her in its tight grip, the kitchen had become a frightening torture chamber in the hills, a circus-funhouse mirror of distortion. A place where what, when and if to eat, or not eat, occupied hours, days—it had been an agony that would seem petty or privileged to someone who didn't understand the hold of the disease. For a long time now, an organized eating schedule and all of the therapy she'd undergone had helped her exist without being in battle with herself and with food, but recollections of the chaos came flooding back to her nonetheless.

"I'm sure the kitchen at your mansion isn't exactly a hob and a hearth," she said quickly, hoping the sound of her own voice would drown out the unwelcome thoughts.

"It's enormous, actually. Several ovens, refrigerators and dishwashers. Easily able to cater parties for a hundred. Of course, it's absurd that it's only for me. Even when Amelia and Lily were there…" His words trailed away while his jaw ticked in the interim. Then he continued, "In any case, it's strictly the domain of the staff. I never step foot in it. I wouldn't have a clue where anything was kept."

"Maybe while you're here we should try to cook the mofongo like we did when Chef Diego gave us our lesson." Dorada was thousands of miles away now, both literally and figuratively.

"I'd love that."

Next, she showed him her bedroom. While she had plenty of other spaces where a guest could stay, even a detached cottage by the pool, she assumed they would share a bed during his time here. Remembering that he didn't sleep well and had set up his own private domain within the open walls of the villa, she pointed to the sequestered alcove in the room that had a desk and chaise lounge that she used to use as an office. "Feel free to make that area yours."

As his eyes scanned the room, she could tell he was as full of apprehension as she was. It had been one thing to talk about him coming to LA and being incorporated into her life, if only for a limited amount of time, but it was quite another to actually do it. They were as awkward as if they'd just met, not acting like two people who'd bared both their souls and their bodies to each other for almost a week. His suit of armor was back on, whereas she felt like one long open wound that hurt to touch. What a pair.

Luna glanced at the bed that the housekeeper had freshly made up for her return. She and Charlie could make love right now. Perhaps that would bring back the ease they'd begun to feel with each other at the villa. Somehow, though, that didn't seem right. She had an idea. "Do you want to go out for a drive?"

They were meandering down a Los Angeles canyon road driven by actress Luna Price in her electric-powered sports car. Had Charlie's famous insomnia played a trick on him yet again? Was he actually hallucinating? From the heat of August in England to the Caribbean steam of Puerto Rico to the arid scorch of the west. His world had been tipped upside down.

"Do you usually drive yourself around town?" he wondered, as she'd spoken so often about the unrelenting attraction of the press to shiny objects such as her. "Surely the tinted windows of a bodyguard's vehicle is more in keeping with the life of a glitterati."

She turned down the rock music she'd been blaring ever since they'd gotten into the car in her covered garage. Explaining that the housekeeper had maintained her cars in her absence, she chose the smaller of the two, the other was an SUV, for their jaunt. Neither were superflashy but he'd still been surprised she kept cars at all. "It's just too unbearable not being able to just hop into a car sometimes and get away. That was an autonomy I wasn't willing to sell. Believe me, the studio will send a car first thing in the morning tomorrow."

He had to admit that Luna looked incredibly sexy as she competently maneuvered the sharp twists and treacherous cliffs of a drive she obviously knew well. With the windows down, her golden waves flew through the air and her unmadeup face glowed. His mouth tipped a private smile at the fun they'd had *dressing her down* for their outing. The exact opposite of when she'd put on her glamazon gear at the resort.

"What do you think?" she'd asked him, emerging from her bedroom closet when they'd decided to go out. In athletic shorts made of a synthetic material, blue with yellow stripes down the sides, coupled with a loose grey T_shirt and sneakers, Luna Price surely did know how to take it down as well as she did to amp it up. In fact, she looked like a skinny young college student in the getup.

"Decidedly less than glamorous, if that's what you were going for," he'd answered with a nod. "And now what, a baseball hat?"

"Mmm, that's a tricky one. The paps are usually on to women in baseball hats. Pick me a wig." She'd pointed to her dressing area, where a shelf held half a dozen wigs on pedestal stands. One was a short, brunette hairstyle. Another, shoulder-length and curly. Another still was long but very dark and stick-straight, unlike her own glorious blond waves.

"How about this one?"

"Grab it. I'll put in on when we get out of the car. And a hat, too." She'd pointed to a rack that held an assortment of styles. He'd chosen a black bucket hat. Then she'd pointed to the door and said, *"Vámanos,"* reminding him that even though she spoke Spanish, no words in any language had been needed when it came to the brazen thrust of his body against hers during those erotic nights at the villa. Charlie still didn't know how he'd let himself end up in Los Angeles. But just as Luna found benefit in time away from an environment that had become unhealthy for her, maybe it was the same for him.

When they arrived onto flat ground at the bottom of the canyon and then drove to the tourist section of Hollywood Boulevard, Charlie guessed where they were going. "I get to see the famous Luna Price's star on the Walk of Fame?"

"You and the ten million who visit annually," she said, stopped at a red light while a countless throng crossed the busy boulevard. She put her arm over her face to block it. Then she turned onto a side street and parked, obviously knowing exactly where her particular star was located.

Once she cut the engine, she looked all around to make sure no one was watching. With the coast clear, she deftly twisted her own hair into a tight spiral and affixed the dark wig to her head. Tilting the rearview mirror toward her, she adjusted and tucked until not one strand of her own lustrous hair was visible. She then topped the wig with the bucket hat Charlie had selected for her. Already wearing sunglasses, her camouflage was complete. Indeed, she didn't look much different than many of the other people strolling down the street. They got out of the car and she tapped her key fob to hear the ping that the doors had been locked.

He was confused by all the quick changes. The movie-star act she had put on at the villa. Now the camouflage just to walk down the street. What about the other her, the flesh and blood of the woman he'd been making love to with all of his might? He couldn't get a footing.

As they walked up to Hollywood Boulevard, she offered some historical perspective on the sidewalk stars. "The first ones were placed on the ground in 1958. Now there are more than two thousand six hundred of them, stretching the length of about a mile."

While Charlie had held meetings in deluxe offices in Century City, browsed the designer shops of Rodeo Drive and eaten cutting-edge tasting menus in the restaurants of celebrity chefs, he'd never just been a tourist on Hollywood Boulevard. Luna rounded the corner, passing businesses peddling everything from pizza to souvenirs. There was even an oddities museum.

"Bus tours to the stars' homes! Bus tours

to the stars' homes!" a hawker yelled out, trying to book seats for his next departure. He called over to Luna, "Would you like to see where the movie stars live, miss?"

"Not this time," she answered politely then snickered to herself.

"Do those people know where you live?" Charlie asked when they were out of earshot.

"Thank heavens, no. It's mostly a scam. Maybe a house where someone stayed a long time ago or where some older star from the Golden Age once lived."

"Feeding in to the Dream Factory."

"Smoke and mirrors, honey." Even though she said it in a mock glam tone, it jarred him that she called him *honey*. Was she just being flippant or was she implying something sincere?

Or maybe he still hadn't met the real Luna yet. And maybe he never would. What if the woman in Puerto Rico was another persona she projected as a way to escape the star label that attracted eyes to her every move? Whereas he thought she was being earnest, it could have been quite the opposite. Perhaps she herself didn't even know what was real. Regret flashed through him, and he questioned if he shouldn't have come here to further unravel her and make things even more complicated for himself.

In front of a taco shop, among other five-pointed stars spaced an equal distance apart all up and down the boulevard's sidewalk, was Luna's.

"Look at that," Charlie said, shaking his head at how surreal the moment was. "Luna Price. Do they all have the emblem of a movie camera under the name?"

"No. That's for people in movies. There are others with television receivers, radio microphones and so on."

"What are they made of?"

"I happen to know! They're constructed from coral-colored terrazzo, which is chipped marble. And the rim, name and emblem are brass."

"Don't they do a big unveiling ceremony when they put in a new one?"

"That was a very special day," she said wistfully. "Before Hollywood started to eat me alive."

"Well, it's an amazing accomplishment."

She smiled as if truly proud. "Thank you. It is."

He handed her his phone. "Take my photo

with it." She complied and then they took selfies with the both of them and the star. The silliness of it all relaxed them and they made funny faces and giggled until their sides ached.

A tour group walked by, distinguishable because they all wore matching laminated cards on red lanyards around their necks. Some diligently checked every star on the walk, perhaps looking for someone in particular.

In front of hers they overheard an exchange. "Luna Price. What ever happened to her? She hasn't worked in a long time."

"I never liked her, anyway."

It was a laugh-or-cry moment. Fortunately, Luna chose the former. They both burst into hysterics and Charlie tugged her down the block.

"Ms. Price." A knock was heard at Luna's trailer door. "We need you in five."

"Thank you," Anush Vardanyan called out as she opened the door a crack. Charlie had met Luna's best friend and employee a couple of hours earlier, when the two women reunited after last being together in Kentucky. He knew it was Anush who'd made the reservation with the M Dating Agency, taking it upon herself to decide the week's transition before going back to work would be just what Luna needed. Charlie wanted to hug the dark-haired young woman dressed all in black for her foresight, as meeting Luna was one of the most important things that had ever happened to him. Anush had also been instrumental in getting her into treatment for her eating disorder in the first place.

"Ms. Price, can you turn your head this way for me?" a makeup artist asked while he added the finishing touches to Luna's heavily painted and powdered face as she sat in the styling chair. She complied.

"Ms. Price, can I get you a little more to the left?" asked the hairdresser, who was working on her locks at the same time, and whose request required Luna to move in the opposite direction the makeup artist had asked for.

"Ms. Price, may I apply one more gloss coat to your nails?" the manicurist chimed in, which forced Luna to extend her hands while her hair and eyelids were being attended to. Now Charlie couldn't see her face from the angle he was sitting at on one of the sofas in her lavishly appointed trailer. But he could see from her reflection in the mirror that all of the primping was taking its toll as her eyebrows were raised and her lips were a straight line. They'd been at it for well over an hour. A protective instinct in him wanted them to stop.

Inside the trailer was a bathroom with a shower, a dining table and chairs in a kitchen area, a high-tech office nook, two sofas facing each other and a huge mounted television monitor. Luna's dressing area held racks of costumes. The makeup chair was in front of mirrors that adjusted to present different angles, and various lighting options.

"Charlie," she said, managing to call out among the tangle of hands on her, "have you ever been to a film set before?"

"No, I haven't."

"Be prepared to be bored. We do things over and over again. There are a lot of people to please."

"I'm sure I'll find it fascinating. Don't forget, I spend my days in front of a computer screen."

During moments of this whirlwind adventure with Luna, Charlie had here and there momentarily forgotten that he ran a huge tech empire in a land called England far, far away, so enthralled had he become with all things Luna.

The lump of coal that he carried in his chest would forever remind him of the past, of the losses that could never be replaced. The sounds that called to him in the night, even here in LA, the pierce of a screaming baby even though Charlie wasn't with his young Lily when the accident took her life. Those voices, he could never run away from. He was checking in with Tom first thing every morning and there were no burning fires and so his mind hadn't really been on business, which was a first in ten years. Was it actually okay for him to take a little more time to rejuvenate? He couldn't convince himself that it wasn't.

When Luna stood up after the ministrations were complete, it was quite the presentation. The movie industry was serious business, and these were professionals at the top of their game. Luna looked…quite simply flawless. Not a hair out of place. Her skin as smooth as a slate of marble. Almost otherworldly. Almost bloodless. Not at all like the animated face that he had laughed so much with that he thought his sides would split on the way home from their jaunt to Hollywood Boulevard yesterday. He still couldn't tell who was really who in this town of artifice.

When they'd gotten back to her house yesterday, Luna had warned him that she needed to get to bed early because she'd be up at dawn. He'd assumed she meant slumber. After a quick dinner they fell into her big comfortable bed to delight in each other, so that she still got to sleep on time, something else they chuckled about.

He'd lain awake and watched over her as she rested, learning the lights and shadows of her bedroom, wondering to himself how long he should stay and what coming here at all might mean. To her. To him. It was all so unexpected, finding in Puerto Rico a bond that seemed like one in a million.

Oh, Amelia, were those kites on that sunny lawn of El Morro really a sign?

"Here we go," Luna said to him now, with a gesture toward the trailer's exit. Anush swung the door open and a muscular handler was there to accompany Luna to set. Charlie, Anush and the glam team followed behind. Charlie was fascinated at the entourage he had become part of. They walked a short distance to the soundstage, a cavernous structure as big and tall as a barn. But once inside, Charlie could see that a set of an office had been constructed.

"Films are shot out of sequence," Anush told him as they entered the stage. "Today, Luna, playing Alice Stephens, is going to be kidnapped by the evil Gaseous Goblin."

"Oh, no, no, no," a booming voice called out. The film's director, Kitt Kormen, a compact man in his thirties who wore a cap backwards on his head, charged over to Luna and her group. "She looks horrible in that dress. Is she hot, or is she a potato sack?"

A costumer rushed over. "Kitt, we approved this in meetings. Do you want to see it with a belt?" Charlie noticed a few members of the crew who were mulling about stopped to watch Kitt's tirade and whispered among themselves.

"I want to see a dress that doesn't make her look like a stone pillar. Can we get something with shape? Is that too much to ask?"

If first impressions were right, Charlie could see why Luna didn't like Kitt. A gentleman might have welcomed a movie star back onto a set after her time away from the cameras. Charlie could see the stress wash over Luna's face, even under all the makeup she wore. She'd told him about this kind of scrutiny regarding her looks. That it was part of the job. A part that she wasn't well able to cope with, and had led her to dysmorphic ideas about her body. A body that Charlie adored touching and tasting and wrapping himself around. A body that was perfect.

While everyone waited for some new dresses to be considered, Luna and the team filed back to the trailer. Anush went to her car and returned with a stack of men's clothes in her arms. "Charlie," she said as she entered the trailer, "Luna said you needed some clothes for your time in LA. We guessed at your size. Do you want to try these on?"

Charlie looked at Luna, who had sat carefully in a chair so as not to muss her hair and makeup. "Oh, so now I'm the one who has to model outfits for approval?"

"Ha," she jeered. "Misery loves company." And they laughed again.

CHAPTER ELEVEN

"So, what is actually going on with you and Charlie?" Anush asked a few days later after entering Luna's trailer. "You didn't tell me you were bringing him back to LA." She set the two iced lattes she'd picked up for them on a table. Luna had been rehearsing some lines before being called to set and was ready for a break. She picked up her drink and with a well-practiced maneuver she was able to get the straw between her teeth so that she could enjoy it without marring her perfectly applied lipstick. They were alone because the beauty squad was out at lunch.

"Puerto Rico wasn't what I was expecting, that's for sure."

"Great."

"You rascal. You were hoping this would

happen when you booked the M Dating Agency trip, weren't you?"

"Guilty as charged. I thought the whole thing would do you good, but what's wrong with letting a man get to know you and not *her*?" Anush emphasized the last word as she swept out her arm, indicating the racks of costume and surfaces strewn with photos of Luna. "That's what resulted, isn't it?"

"Oh," Luna said on a whoosh of breath. "I don't know. It's complicated. He lost his wife and child. He'll never get over his heartache. It's all fun and fine now, but what about the long run?"

"Anybody could say that about any relationship. You can't predict the future."

"It's just that when I was in therapy, there was a lot of talk about me taking care of me. And keeping the focus on that."

"What are you afraid of?"

Luna took another sip of her drink. "I feel like I'm falling in love with him." She let the words settle all around her to decide if they were true. Which they were. She absolutely adored having Charlie here at the studio and with her at night. She could have never guessed at the security that would make her feel. He'd flown up to Silicon Valley today and she was looking forward to his return. He was going to accompany her to a film premiere tonight. She was in such a better mental state that even Kitt's tantrums were easy to keep in perspective. Charlie was the unforeseen element that Luna hadn't known was missing.

But she was afraid of a crash. She was afraid of counting on anyone. Afraid that she didn't know how to trust. What if she ruined it by being too needy? Or not needy enough? Afraid of the words he'd said, that he'd never love again, plain and simple, for fear he couldn't withstand any more heart-break.

"Why is falling in love a bad thing?" Anush persisted. "I want to fall in love. Doesn't everybody?"

"I don't think he'll be able to do it again." Especially if he stayed in LA much longer. He was not part of this artificial world that was her stock and trade. He was a quiet man and even though that was something she felt so calm and comfortable around, the reality was that she had a loud life.

"So you'll take it one step at a time."

"Stop being so optimistic," Luna teased.

"Isn't that why you keep me around?"

Anush smiled back. "So, what are you wearing tonight?"

And suddenly, as one of the most glamorous women in the world, she was reduced to a giggly teenager who wanted to look cute for her prom date.

Judging from Charlie's response, she succeeded. Anush had helped her pick out a slinky green dress that Luna secretly favored over the others because it matched the color of Charlie's eyes. It was sleeveless and with a neckline that made a *V* so low it almost reached her waist. In fact, Anush employed the Hollywood magic of double-sided tape to keep it from becoming scandalous when Luna moved.

In his slim-cut black suit, no doubt bespoke from the finest tailor London had to offer, Charlie was knee-bucklingly handsome. Which was good, because he could have no idea of the inspection that was about to take place. When the driver brought him to the studio, where Luna had dressed after wrapping the shoot for the day, the look on Charlie's face was classic. Like a cartoon rabbit whose eyes popped from their sockets and bounced outward on springs. His lascivious glance started at her exposed throat and made its way slowly, ever so slowly, at that, down the open expanse of her chest until his eyes settled where the fabric finally came together just above her waist. Even though he'd told her many times that he liked her naked and natural better than in any of the other guises she wore, she had to admit that she liked looking sexy when she was about to introduce him to the world as her man.

Even though the studios, and her team, had often paired her up with someone for public appearances, it had never felt like an organic date. Yes, on occasion she'd spent the night with one of them at a hotel afterward, but dawn had always brought out selfish ambitions or opportunistic efforts that she saw right through. Like when she'd been tricked by Troy Lutt, who was out to make a buck off her mistake in being with him. Being driven home up the hill, alone, on those mornings after had been the most hollow and lonely Luna had ever felt, and often led to those horrible internal battles about her body and food.

So for the first time, she was going to arrive at a big Hollywood event on the arm of a man she cared about. A tiny worry about being drained dry again by the bloodthirsty press percolated within her, though, and she didn't know how Charlie would respond to the limelight. After all, he'd come to Puerto Rico to get ready to put on his own public face after so many years in isolation. But Hollywood was no place for a slow start; it was straight into the frying pan.

Still, part of her was excited to reclaim her place as one of the queens of Tinseltown. She deserved a comeback with all of the fanfare. After the driver pulled to the curb where the red carpet began, he came around to open the door for them. Charlie stepped out first and turned to extend his arm to help Luna out. As soon as she emerged, the screams of her name began. She took Charlie's arm and they turned to face the crowd side by side. But he didn't manage the proud and privileged smile she needed him to beam to the camera. Instead, the massive barrage of flashing camera lights were so bright that Charlie quickly jerked his arm up to cover his eyes from their blinding burn.

Luna's New Man! The world's best-known celebrity-watching site graphics were big

and bold on the screen across a photo of
Luna and Charlie from the night before.
Over early morning orange juice and pea-
nut butter on toast at her white breakfast
table, Charlie was reading out loud to her
from his tablet. Switching to another site, he
read . "'Luna Price's return to Hollywood
after an unexplained absence included the
first viewing of what looks to be a romantic liaison. Sources identified the mystery
man as Charlie Matthews, British billionaire
who founded the wildly successful biotech
firm AMgen at the tender age of nineteen.
Hats off to the jolly chap who captured Luna's heart.'"

"Jolly chap?" Luna looked up from the
script she was half studying. "They think
they're being cutely British with that? That's
cheap, even for them."

"Ugh, how can you bear this crap?" Charlie paused for a swig of his juice, then tapped
on another article. "'Matthews could star in
his own drama, which would be a weeper,
as ten years ago his young wife and child
were killed in a car accident.'"

His hands dropped from the keyboard.
His face turned ashen. It was as though a
still thickness had fogged the air.

"Oh, Charlie," Luna murmured, barely above a whisper. "I'm so sorry. These gossipmongers are completely soulless. They'd sell their own mother for a story." This was exactly what she'd feared. That the brutality of the world she inhabited would cause him harm. She'd chosen this—the bad with the good was a trade-off. But he didn't belong, and there was no benefit to him being stripped of his privacy and dignity.

"Apparently," he mumbled back. Before he could go further, she asked to see his tablet. For two reasons. One, he didn't need to read anything else that might make mention of the personal trauma that had defined his adult life. And secondly, she figured she'd take her pain straight up and get it over with. She punched in the addresses for the fashion sites that would have been at the premiere last night in droves.

It didn't take her long to find what she knew she would.

"'Luna, trying hard to reestablish her big place in the film industry with an unfortunately small swath of a dress.'

"'Looking like a four-leaf clover, Luna might be lucky in love but will win no pot of gold for her neon-green dress better suited to a teen pop star.'

"'Only someone like Luna, who has no curves, could pull off the engineering feat required to keep that dress up.'"

Her gut began to bubble.

Is she hot, or is she a potato sack? Kitt's comment from her first day on set replayed in her head.

Only someone like Luna, who has no curves...

And then she found yet another site that had caught a photo of them that first day, unbeknownst to her, on Hollywood Boulevard. "'What is Luna hiding under those baggy clothes and wig? Did visiting her own star give her a needed ego boost?'"

There it all was, just as she had left it a year ago. The press's unending cravings. It didn't even seem to matter if it was true information or not. They wanted to assume, insinuate, guess. All the old feelings gurgled back. That her success hadn't really been earned, but it had been granted. She could be a glittery enough object that held fascination, but only if she was constantly vigilant. Being perfect all the time was the only formula, yet perfection was subjective. How could she please everybody all the time? Therapy had taught her that she couldn't. But something was stuck between her intellect and her emotions. Which is what had led her to make mistakes and keep secrets. Secrets she held tightly, silently, in the dark rooms of her mind until they almost killed her.

And now she'd brought Charlie into the wreckage. How foolish she'd been, in the throes of seduction, underneath a magical waterfall on a faraway island, to ask him to come into this zombie feeding frenzy of her life. This was a side of the real her that nobody would want to be around. She pushed away her plate of toast, no longer hungry.

"My car will be here soon," she said softly. "Do you want to come to the studio with me today?"

Expecting him to say no, she was relieved when he agreed.

"Yes. I've got some work to attend to, but I can do it there." His eyes were dull, but he bravely stood to get ready.

Kitt and the screenwriters decided to make a couple of dialogue changes, so Luna spent a lot of the day waiting. She sent Anush home and banished the squad from her trailer until needed. Had she or Charlie been in a better mood, they could have played a card game or something to pass the time. But the morning's headlines still resonated through her, and she suspected Charlie was second-guessing everything, as well.

"The phone call came at eleven fifty-six in the evening," he said, eyes fixed on the painting of a tree above the table.

"What call?"

"The police. To tell me that an accident had occurred. They told me there was no point in me coming to the scene as they'd be rushing the victims to the hospital. I have almost no recollection of running through the house to get to the car, only of myself driving in the dead of an icy night." Luna looked around her trailer. The shoes that cost thousands of dollars. The styling chair where a half-dozen people made their livelihood by servicing an industry of make-believe. Nothing mattered at all in the face of Charlie's tragedy. "It was Lily's six-month birthday. That would indeed make for a tear-jerker of a film, wouldn't it?"

Tears rolled down Luna's cheeks. She didn't care if her makeup artist was going to have to start his work over again today. Her heart shattered for Charlie. She reached for his hand, which was next to hers on the sofa. He accepted it, but distractedly. With her other hand, she stroked his forearm up and down, down and up, hoping to soothe him in some way. A small crook of his lip told her he had noticed.

When she was finally called for a quick reshoot, Charlie followed along, perhaps just for the activity. The sun had already gone down and a fair amount of the crew had been dismissed. So, unusually, a handler wasn't sent to accompany Luna the short distance to set.

As soon as they stepped out of the trailer, she heard it. *Click, click, click, click.* Rapid-fire, like bullets from a machine gun. Someone with a long-lensed camera was in the vicinity. *Click, click, click.* The sound would be forever etched in her brain. On and on it went. Whoever the photographer was would take hundreds of shots, hoping for the one good one that would make a sale to the tabloids. Charlie, with tension in his eyes after reliving the night that altered him forever, heard it, too. He whipped his head around and located the camera being focused on them. The glower he pierced the photographer with could have curdled blood.

The next morning, he checked his phone and showed it to her. Sure enough, there was a photo of Charlie seething, with Luna by his side, the reason for his scowl misconstrued. The caption read, Luna Price's new love affair—already on the rocks?

Charlie walked Luna out her front door and waved her off as the driver took her to the studio. He'd had enough of being trapped in her trailer, which seemed even more of a fortress now that he'd witnessed the relentless paparazzi, who perched like vultures everywhere she went, planning their attack, always ready. That Luna could withstand their constant presence was hard to believe. In a way he felt proud of her, proud that she ultimately must have a very strong character to stand up to all of that limelight. He knew it had gotten to her, which is why she'd taken the year off. He hoped, for her sake, that her recovery tools would be enough to keep her from sliding back into danger.

She'd suggested he take one of her cars and go out to the beach while she worked,

promising that they'd meet tonight for a
low-key dinner at home. Sensible advice,
and perhaps a drive to the ocean would do
him good. He still couldn't shake the bloodthirsty face of that photographer yesterday,
the vicious glee he took in snapping shots
when he shouldn't have. Not long after Luna
left, Charlie got into her car and flipped the
ignition. Swooshing down the canyon was
exhilarating and he cranked up the rock 'n'
roll Luna had programmed.

The Pacific Ocean was as fierce as he
remembered it, with tall waves exploding
onto the shoreline. The waters surrounding
sweet Puerto Rico were so much milder by
comparison. He parked the car and walked
down the path leading to the beach. It was
still morning and the beachcombers were
just beginning to stake their claims in the
sand with blankets, picnics, toys and towels. A windy morning, at that, which is why
he watched a few people struggle to anchor
the poles of their umbrellas.

He took off his shoes, rolled up his pants
and went as far as ankle-deep into the brac-
ingly cold water, where he began his stroll.
He thought of Luna's luminous face under
the tender moon of Puerto Rico.

Luna, Luna. With her, he'd begun to think that energy could whoosh through his veins again. She'd reawakened him sexually, made him virile and potent once more, able to howl into those sultry Caribbean midnights. Together they'd looked into the mirror and been willing to face what they saw. For a brief moment in time, Charlie thought he could change that reflection from a man whose heart and soul and spirit had already been used up into someone whose well was full again. Who had hope.

But his central nervous system told him otherwise. He'd put a tiny crack in that hard shell, certain that he'd now be able to manage a dinner date or attend a party under the guise of civilized society. Puerto Rico let in just a sliver of light so that he could appease his employees and his investors. Progress had been made. That was enough.

He couldn't survive at Luna's level of interaction with the human race. She deserved someone who could. Someone who could even rise above it to put boundaries around the invasion. Charlie had built a wall around himself, but the space was only large enough for him. In Puerto Rico, he'd thought for a minute he might be able to tear down the barriers and truly live out in the open, in trust, in faith. The last few days in LA had shown him how wrong he'd been.

He kicked the sand and shook his head. A family playing on the beach caught his eye. The woman and the littlest ones filled colorful plastic containers with sand. An older girl, probably about ten, the same age Lily would have been if she was still alive, and her father were trying to fly kites. Amelia and her kites. The vivid displays of kites at the El Morro in Viejo San Juan. Charlie had convinced himself that they were a sign from Amelia, assuring him that not only could he smile again, but also that he could love once more.

In this morning's swirling wind, the girl and her father couldn't get the kites into the air. They floundered, flopping over and over in the sand, the lines tangling into a mess. That was the real sign, Charlie thought to himself. Not being able to fly the kite. Not even getting it off the ground.

CHAPTER TWELVE

"LUNA, SIT UP STRAIGHTER!" Kitt yelled over as he and his cinematographer, Hans, viewed her through several camera lenses.

"The shoulders are still off."

"And I don't like the shadow under the chin."

"You're slouching, Luna. Can you *please* sit up straighter?"

"I can blend out some of the width here and here." Hans gestured something to Kitt.

Luna could feel the simmer within her. It always began as little bubbles in her gut, like a fountain just beginning to gurgle. Making her feel restless, uncomfortable in her own skin. Listening to the two men talk about *the shoulders* and *the chin*, as if she was a collection of inanimate parts, the bubbles were multiplying. They made her want to sink down into the spring so that their words couldn't reach her. It was starting again. She knew it as sure as she'd know night from day.

She and Charlie had spent the day apart. He texted that he'd gone to the beach. Things weren't right between them—they could both feel it in their bones. They were a million miles from the carefree shores of Puerto Rico. Him being in LA wasn't working out.

That night, Luna was detained on set for so long that by the time she got home, she'd missed the dinner they were planning. She found Charlie asleep on one of the living room sofas, the golden glow from a lamp obscuring half of his face. Knowing that sleep didn't come easy for him, she wasn't about to disturb him, so she covered him with a blanket and turned off the light.

She'd already had both the assistant director and her manager tell Kitt that she needed to keep reasonable hours if she was going to do her best work. Last time she'd approached Kitt herself, he'd reminded her that after she'd disappeared last year, throwing off the production schedule for the film and costing the studio millions of dollars, she might want to be less demanding. She remembered in therapy discussing how to circumvent people who pressed her buttons. Wisely, she'd decided not to have any conversations directly with Kitt anymore. But it had been a trying day. She forced herself to eat a sandwich and then got into her own bed, alone.

In the morning, she promised Charlie a rain check on dinner. And so indeed, before the moon had risen too high in the sky that night, she and Charlie sat at her kitchen table for a home-cooked meal, albeit one prepared by her housekeeper.

"You haven't touched your food," he observed.

The bubbles began to percolate inside her again. She hated people noticing or commenting on what she ate. Pausing, she realized that he was only trying to help.

She picked up her fork and knife, then sliced into the roast chicken with a seasoning rub she'd asked her housekeeper to prepare. Bringing the bite to her mouth, the spices reminded her of lovemaking in the sand and of Charlie's smile, which she hadn't seen in days.

She followed one bite with another. As they'd talked about in therapy, if she took the right actions then the right thinking would follow.

"It doesn't seem as if things are going well on the film."

"Perhaps I came back to a movie set too soon," she replied, voicing what she'd been thinking. "This week is triggering me. I thought I was further along in my recovery."

"I know what you mean. What we shared at Dorada made me think for the first time since my family's death that I might be able to start again with someone new," he said, eyes cast down on his dinner plate and not on her. But then he lifted them. "Not with *someone*. With you."

"But?"

"I can't smile for the cameras. I can't put makeup over the wounds that still burn me until I'm red and chapped every single night. Yes, I'll rise up enough to do what I need to do to keep AMgen growing and thriving, even if I'm not. But I think that's all I'll ever be able to manage."

"I don't know if I can smile for the cameras anymore, either. Even though I used to be a master at disguising who I really was inside. I was more of an actress in my personal life than I ever was on the silver screen. I'm not sure it's worth it anymore. I have some more soul-searching to do."

They finished eating in silence. Was he thinking what she was? About what might have been? The American movie star and the British tech billionaire. Two damaged people finding each other in the darkness and hanging on for dear life was the stuff fantasies were made of. Because kindred spirits don't come around every day. Because the safety, comfort and chances they found in each other's arms was too rare and precious a gift to let go of.

But that wasn't their script.

"It's time for me to go home to England."

Sorrow manifested in one tear that made a slow slide down Luna's face. "I know."

Charlie had never hated a flight more. As his jet rocketed him through the clouds, he squeezed his eyes shut for a minute. It was as if the week in Puerto Rico and this second one in California had happened in a trance. Like a vision, from which he was supposed to emerge from and then forget, getting on with his life, until the details faded away like the vast county of Los Angeles, with its endless suburbs and swimming pools that looked like little dots of turquoise viewed from the sky.

When his regular driver picked him up at Heathrow in London, his familiar face confirmed that Charlie was indeed home. The route to his estate was one he'd traveled many times, although his driver's voice sounded tinny and distant.

The entrance hall looked like a mausoleum today. Which, in essence, it was. For ten years Charlie had considered it a cemetery, one he'd refused to leave. As if staying in the house kept Amelia and Lily nearer to him, and he was watching over his family, even though their remains were in the ground miles away. Images of Luna's skirt as she danced the bomba and all that had transpired between them paraded in front of him, a vision from another lifetime. The tombstones were the only things that were real.

While he sifted through the mail on his desk, he could only think of Luna. First viscerally, of her silken skin and lush lips and sweet smell, like sugar in the sun. The unbridled eroticism they shared was shocking. His hunger, his sovereignty, his want for her breathed a charge back into him. But it was more than that. Even though he and Amelia had enjoyed fulfilling lovemaking, he'd been just a young adult then. Not yet in touch with his own physical prowess. Not even knowing he was capable of a savage fervor that scorched the earth he and Luna traversed. What they'd unlocked within each other was life-changing. He'd never be the same man. As he brought his luggage into the foyer for his housekeeper to unpack tomorrow, an empty thud of finality beat in his chest.

He and Luna had also knocked into a stunning candor with each other. Perhaps it was the nature of the setup through the M Dating Agency. They were both people who needed a passageway to whatever was next. Even though Charlie might never be able to exorcise the haunts of this house, he felt different indeed, although perhaps not in the ways he'd have expected. Would Luna defeat her own enemies? For a brief moment he thought they might be able to trudge on their paths side by side. But no, he'd have to walk alone. The pain of a fresh solitude needled up his spine.

There was that something between them that couldn't be put into words. Lying on top of her, their bodies speaking in the most intimate way possible, their solar plexuses met, as well. The auras that emanated from each of them into the ether had become one. There was no separation of his spirit from hers. It was a tie he'd never known anything of, not even with Amelia. He was only able to receive it after earning the maturity he held now. Unfortunately, he dared not trust it. Because if he was wrong, if their synthesis was only born of circumstance and loneliness, it could easily betray him or evaporate. He couldn't withstand any more defeat.

Had he hurt Luna by deciding to leave LA? It was with a flat resignation that they both agreed the M encounter, as planned, and the unplanned week in LA were all they would have together. Clearly, her year away from the spotlight hadn't sorted all of her issues. She needed to get right within herself. But a voice within him screamed that they could have helped each other conquer it all. He hated himself for not being able to try. She was where the light shone. Without her, everything was dim. His palms flattened against the cold walls of his stone corridor as he made his way to his empty bed.

"Good to see you." Tom greeted Charlie with a firm handshake at the shareholders' meeting the next day.

"I can't promise I'm a changed man in every respect, but I understand what I have to do." He'd been dutifully shaking hands with guests for an hour. It was exhausting.

"Not changed 'in every respect.' What does that mean? What happened? Charlie, I have to say that I was hopeful when you decided to extend the trip and go to LA."

"Hopeful about what?"

"That in Luna you'd unexpectedly met someone you might create a future with."

"Perhaps I bit off more than I could chew there."

"Did you find out that you and Luna weren't compatible, despite M's careful matchmaking skills?"

"Quite the opposite."

"Then what are you waiting for? Amelia and Lily have been gone ten years. Are you going to mourn for your entire life?"

"Believe me, I ask myself the same question all the time."

"Tell me about her."

"Luna? She's marvelous. Vibrant and smart and thoughtful. I'll cherish our time together for the rest of my life. Thank you for setting that up," he said wistfully. He honestly didn't know if he wanted to thank Tom or hate him. For showing him what he could have had if he'd been able to reach out and grab it. That was like taunting a hungry man with food but not letting him eat.

"I read something philosophical not long ago that said something to the effect of when you're lying on your deathbed, it's nothing you did—like eating that chocolate mousse, or taking that impulsive trip to Prague, or telling someone you loved them—that you'll have remorse over. It's the things you didn't do for which you'll have regret."

That night, he sat on his oxblood leather chair sipping a brandy in front of his unlit fireplace like an old man. Was he at the end of his life? That wasn't fair to him. That wasn't fair to his memories or to Luna. He had to tear down the stone walls. Earlier, Tom had inferred what Charlie already knew. That he loved Luna. Dearly. Urgently. Wholeheartedly. LA had cast doubt in him about who Luna was. Was she the humble rancher's daughter or the Hollywood star millions admired? The fragile creature that crumbled under pressure or the warrior who put herself back together? But he'd realized that she was all of those things. And more. He wanted to hold dear every precious facet of her. Embrace it all. Forever.

"Wake up, sleepyhead." Anush's voice came through Luna's phone once she'd swiped it open after hearing the ringtone of Puerto Rican drumbeats.

"I'm not due on set to…" She stopped herself, remembering that she wasn't shooting with Kitt. She had a TV appearance today. A film that was finished a year and a half ago was finally being released and she had a press interview to promote it. "Oh, right. I have to be *her* again this morning."

A flicker of anxiety pinged through her. Would she look good enough? Would the camera operator be one who flattered or was careless? She mentally reviewed her talking points.

"I've got the tan-colored suit for you with the midnight blue blouse if you're still feeling good about that," Anush offered.

"Which shoes?"

"The brown slingbacks."

"Okay." Luna moaned and stretched like a cat. She didn't want to get out of bed and face the morning, but she had to.

"Why don't you bring Charlie along? That ought to make the day sweeter." Silence. "I'm winking even though you can't see it."

Silence again.

"Luna?" Anush coaxed.

"Charlie went back to England."

"Why?"

"There was no point in him staying."

The night before last, they'd agreed that they weren't going to be able to turn the magic they'd found at Dorada into something long-lasting. Luna had been due early on set again yesterday, so she'd gone to bed. She'd sensed Charlie all night on the chaise in the alcove she'd assigned as his space. His rustling told her that he hadn't slept much, either. In the morning, they were like professionals who had completed a deal. They thanked each other for the time they'd shared. He gave her a matter-of-fact kiss on the cheek before slipping into the back seat of the car he'd arranged to take him the airport. Luna, barefoot and in a thin pink robe, had stood outside and watched the car take the curves in the road away from her house before she let her tears fall.

"Luna, you're one of the most glittering stars on the planet. Men find you beautiful. Women want to be you. What is it *you* want?"

Charlie. She wanted Charlie. Nothing had ever felt as good as being with him in Puerto Rico had. There, she felt safe. Accepted. Looked after but respected at the same time. Heard.

She hadn't been able to keep that fire kindled once they got back to LA. The pressure was too much. It was understandable. She'd just returned from a year away, when she'd learned to manage her shadows. How to see them for what they were. To circumvent negative thoughts before they turned into destructive behaviors. She was a work in progress but she'd made leaps and bounds from where she was a year ago, when she'd hidden in that dark place of denial, alone, keeping secrets.

Of course, she could see in hindsight that it had been too much to bring Charlie into that complex fold before she'd even had a chance to sort it out. Yet they couldn't haved said goodbye at Dorada. What they'd shared there was too special, they'd come to mean too much to each other. It was an honest mistake of hers to invite him here, but a mistake nonetheless.

Maybe someday she would have enough distance from the phony priorities that had brought her down and she could think about finding a man who didn't care when the public inevitably moved on to the next pretty face. Perhaps after her star had faded she could find someone to live out a companionable existence with. Although she'd always know that she let *the one* slip away because she'd convinced herself she wasn't ready for him. Anguish overtook her until she could barely breathe. Logic didn't make sense. There was only her heart aching to put her hand in his and trudge the road as one. Was someone ever ready for love?

Love.

She was in love with Charlie. The words bounced from left to right, front to back in her mind. In love. In. Love. It was an active state, present tense. In. Love. The most amazing thing that had ever happened to her. And yet he was over five thousand miles away and out of her life.

* * *

The crew at the taping studio where Luna was to do her interview had her sit every which way while they adjusted lights and sound. The interviewer, Blick Jenson, host of a widely watched entertainment news program, was known for pushing outside of the agreed-upon topics. As it was, her emotions were raw, so she was apprehensive, and would remain on guard until the segment was over. Once they began, as an actress she easily spoke with enthusiasm about the role that had actually bored her to tears. She had only complimentary things to say about yet another director who had made her feel like a plastic doll under his command.

True to form, Blick began probing. "Luna, we haven't seen you in a year. Will you share with us where you've been and why you took a break from Hollywood?"

Definitely not a subject on the approved list. She bristled, resentful at him for not following the rules of respect, for putting her on the spot. Luna's management team had decided that absolutely nothing would be said about her absence. She'd simply pick up where she left off and the public's curiosity would die down soon enough. Movies were released on all sorts of odd schedules relative to when they were shot, and she'd swiftly make up for lost time.

Yet as she was about to pivot his question to something safer, that bubbling fountain in her belly began to fizz. Only this time it wasn't because her eating disorder was possessing her body, about to make her undo all of the hard work she'd done in Kentucky. No, it was quite the opposite. Those bubbles had become her power. Her truth.

Charlie. How much she'd learned from him! He was incapable of pretending, whereas Luna was a master at pretend. He was who he was while Luna had made a fortune being anyone except herself. But no longer.

"I haven't shared this before," she told Blick, whose eyes widened as he leaned forward from his chair opposite her with interest. Of course, he was as bloodthirsty as the rest, eager for an exclusive scoop. "I was in treatment…for an eating disorder."

The crew, from electrician to lighting tech to makeup artist, froze in their tracks. A pin dropping would have sounded like thunder.

But the words had already fallen out of Luna's mouth. There was no stopping now. Nor did she want to. This would be the next phase of her healing. No longer in the shadows. She continued, "Those of us in front of the cameras are very blessed to be in our professions. When people think of celebrities, they often imagine us as having perfect lives, and looking perfect while having them. Moviemakers deliver to the public a fantasy, a getaway from real life and human problems. Representing that escape took its toll on me. I became sick with anorexia nervosa. Once I realized how bad it had gotten and how much I needed help, I went into a recovery program."

As the hush continued to permeate the set, Blick asked more and more questions until Luna had told him, and the entire world, everything there was to tell. It was absolutely cathartic. Her lungs expanded, her vision sharpened. It was one of the crowning moments of her life, especially when she considered that her confession might be able to help others who were struggling with eating disorders to come out from the dark. If she'd been able to hold a torch for even one person's path, her entire position of fame was worthwhile. She wouldn't let the world judge her for who she was anymore and a feeling of freedom swept over her like a bird in the wind of a limitless sky.

It was almost peace. But there was something essential missing. Something that she'd never find true tranquility or inner wellness without. Something that was six feet tall with nakedly green eyes, and whose embrace gave her those wings. That was another truth that had become clear on this day of candor. She was entitled to a pure and healthy relationship. One where she could love and be loved with complete sincerity. That's what she wanted. She wasn't going to let her fame, or her eating disorder, take that from her. She'd never experienced anything even close to the joy and honesty she'd had with Charlie. She didn't have to live without it and she wasn't going to.

CHAPTER THIRTEEN

"MEET ME BACK at the villa," Charlie demanded. It was dawn in Buckinghamshire, which meant late at night in Los Angeles. But he hadn't been able to wait even one day to place the call that his gut had been fighting for.

"Charlie?"

"When can you take a few days off from filming?"

Standing out on the stone terrace outside of his bedroom, he surveyed the gardens and grounds of his property. The estate had come back to life all of a sudden, even though that wasn't literally possible. It was he who had reignited his own light inside and that made everything look brighter. His grass was the greenest green and the marble was a reflection of his inner gleam. The trees had never been taller, the pond was shimmering, the ducks stately. This home that he had bought to raise a family in had waited for him. During all the grey years, when he'd shuffled like an automaton up and down the polished halls, the house never gave up. Now, all the curtains were drawn back again. Sunshine filled the rooms, and soon the leaves would fall, followed by the winter snow, before spring would bloom anew once again. Charlie wasn't going to be in a daze for even one moment of it. Every leaf would have his full attention. Because he was in love again.

"Let's talk about it at the café in Viejo San Juan, where we ate the grilled eggplant with honey." He thought of how sultry Luna was in those Taino earrings he'd bought and how he couldn't take his hands off her. What he hadn't realized then was that she held his heart in her hand. And always would.

"I'm glad you called. I had this interview and—"

"Yes, I saw it!" Which was why he couldn't wait another minute to talk to her. He'd been all but bursting open with pride. "I want to hear every detail about it. In person. Tell that pipsqueak of a director that you have a personal matter that needs immediate attention. I'll send my plane tomorrow."

"As it happens, during the next few days Kitt is shooting some action sequences that, of course, I'm not in."

"Oh, I could kiss that little weasel after all. I'll arrange all of your transportation. See you at the villa." He tapped off the call with his skin tingling.

When Luna stepped onto the plane at the private hangar at LAX, her jaw dropped open. "Charlie! What are doing here? I thought I was meeting you at Dorada."

"I thought so, too. Until I realized that meant I'd have to wait seven extra hours to see you. So I decided to come get you myself." Charlie had been standing just inside the entrance door so that Luna wouldn't see him until she boarded the plane.

His flight crew milled about but smiled at the prank. They must have sensed his excitement and the sea change within him. Though he'd never been an ogre, he was probably unpleasant to be around as he traversed the globe when AMgen business demanded it, but never with any gusto for travel. Never any gusto for anything.

Once Luna stepped all the way into the cabin, the crew backed away and Charlie threw his arms around her waist, lifted her off the ground and twirled her in a circle. "By the way, I love you," he said into her ear, having forced himself to wait until they were in person to utter those three crucial words.

She leaned back her head and stared at him with those clear blue eyes. "You do?"

Talking to himself in the moment, he fought not to feel rejected by her lack of *I love you, too.* His exuberance was probably not what she expected, and she hadn't known all of the conclusions that had become clear to him once he'd returned to England. It would be all right, he counseled himself. Once they got back to the villa everything would fall into place.

After the flight took off, the attendants brought out an extravagant meal of lobster to start, followed by a creamy pasta, but as they flew across the US, he could tell Luna was regarding him with caution. Like she was deciding something. He didn't like it. He'd become so confident and sure of his feelings for her. It would have been so much easier if she'd been able to do the same. But he could wait, he kept reassuring himself. He'd been getting ready for her for ten years, he just hadn't realized it. What were a few more days, or even weeks?

While they watched a movie to pass the time, Luna dozed off. Then after using the plane's grandly appointed bathroom, she emerged freshened up. He stared deep into her eyes, hoping the love that was overflowing within him would radiate around them and flow inside her. Instead of the smile he'd hoped to receive, though, her mouth flattened into a straight line as she sat down next to him.

"What's wrong?"

"I just don't know if I can have someone look at me the way you do."

"Why?"

"Because what if you stop? What happens when you see a side of me you don't like? When I'm too boring for you? I don't want to get accustomed to someone showering me with care like that."

"Well, you'd better get used to it. Because I'm going to be doing it for the rest of our lives."

Her brow furrowed.

It was okay. He'd show her. He'd have to.

"Welcome back to Recurso Llave Dorada," the manager, Juan Carlos, exclaimed as he ushered Luna and Charlie into the golf cart. Motoring along the familiar path that led to La Villa de Felicidad, Luna flushed with striking memories of the private fantasy world she and Charlie had created. She closed her eyes. The resort did have a particular smell like nowhere else, of fragrant plants native to the area, and Charlie's warm arm pressed against her was divine. The sea air running through her hair made her feel at one with the island.

Once Juan Carlos departed after unloading their luggage, Charlie wrapped an arm around Luna's waist and brought her to him for a homecoming kiss that pulled her up on her toes. While they'd kissed on the plane, they hadn't been alone. Now the privacy of the villa was theirs once more. Her arms wound around his neck before she'd asked them to, so instinctive was her draw to him. Birds chirped in the background as they kissed and then kissed some more.

In fact, it was the most natural thing in

the world when he picked her up into his arms and carried her to the master bedroom, where they had given themselves to one another in every way. Clothes flew off and the plush bedding was tossed back. Luna didn't know where her hands and mouth wanted to go first, she longed for him so. Running the tip of her tongue down the length of his neck, the familiar taste of his skin was spicy and salty and sweet all at once. The moan coming from his vocal cords vibrated against her lips. His sound excited her further, thrumming in her core, driving her. They brought each other to the clouds before collapsing, breathless for the moment. After a while Charlie dozed off, giving Luna immense satisfaction that his body and mind were resting.

Lying in his arms, though, trepidation was a cruel overseer, making sure Luna didn't completely relax. This was now the third go-round with Charlie in only three weeks' time. In LA, after the interview, she'd been secure that she was ready to keep Charlie as hers forever. Once she boarded his plane, however, she wasn't so sure. It hit her that they'd somehow met both the best and the worst of each other but nothing in the middle. What would the realities of the day-in-and-day-out pain he'd always carry look like and how would she manage a lifetime commitment to keep the monster that lived inside of her caged? What if they gave one another their all, but they couldn't make their partnership work? Both stood the chance of total destruction. Now she was filled with uncertainty. She stared at the ceiling, chewing on her lip.

That night, they had a late dinner in the courtyard. Charlie was barefoot, in a loose linen shirt and pants that swayed a bit with the breeze—he looked like the picture of easygoing handsomeness. Not only liberated from the suits and ties his prominence and power dictated, but also shorn of the hipster clothes he'd worn in LA to blend into her world. Which version was the real him, after a fortnight had rocked their old selves to the ground?

"You haven't told me how your interview was received," Charlie said and then reached across the table to take one of her hands in his.

"Kitt was livid, of course. Why should

the focus be on my well-being while he was shooting a blockbuster I didn't even mention? Likewise, I was supposed to be promoting a film I shot ages ago, not talking about my personal transformation."

"Why am I not surprised?"

"My team was in shock, too, that I talked about it so openly after we'd had several meetings to discuss the strategy and I had agreed with the decision not to mention my eating disorder at all."

"What changed your mind?"

She paused. Had a sip of the sparkling water that had been poured into a stemmed glass. The answer she was going to give was complete and accurate. "You."

Charlie's mouth hitched into a grin. "Me?"

"You showed me that it's okay to be who I am. You make me feel like I don't owe anyone anything except my authentic self."

"And how did the public react to that?" Reassuringly, he stroked the top of her hand back and forth with the pad of his thumb.

"Social media went crazy. It was one of the top trending topics."

"Positive or negative?"

"Both. One contingent appreciating that I shed light on an important subject that affects hundreds of thousands of people. Once I calmed my publicist down, I got her to post eating-disorder helplines and links for people reading who might be in need."

"That's wonderful. How could there be anything but praise for your courage?"

"Are you kidding me?"

"What do you mean?"

She picked up her phone and scrolled.

Luna Price, who has made a fortune on her enviably svelte physique, now tells Hollywood that it's put too much pressure on her. Talk about biting the hand that doesn't feed you.

It's somehow someone else's fault that Luna Price can't live up to her own image. The typical self-obsession that makes movie stars into clichés.

Why didn't she try eating a pizza, gaining five pounds and noticing that no one cares?

"Oh, my love. We'll file lawsuits."

She chuckled. "You can't sue people on social media for writing insulting things."

"It's defamation of character."

"You want to hear the strangest thing? I don't even care about the response to what I said."

"You don't?"

"I really don't. I've spent so many years trying to please everyone and racing to stay on top. Like everything is some mountain you have to claw your way to the top of." He brought her hand to his mouth and kissed the top of it. "I'm just done."

"What does that mean?"

Good question. She thought out loud. "I'm done being perfect. Done caring what other people think." And done coming up with reasons why she couldn't have what most people dream of. "And I'm done with a life you're not in. I love you, Charlie."

Without letting go of her hand, he stood, bringing her up with him so they could embrace under the moon. "And I'll tell you something else," she continued, fired up. "A year wasn't long enough away from Hollywood for me to really get my health back. Might you have a spare room at your mansion?" Their lips met in a joining that Luna now knew was her home.

* * *

Charlie swung his hips with the abandon he remembered from when they were here last time. The groove got under Luna's skin, too, and she flitted the ruffles of her skirt while she fixed a seductive gaze on him until he thought he'd melt like hot candle wax. He wanted nothing more than to dance this night away with her in Viejo San Juan. No, that wasn't true. What he wanted was to dance with her every night.

"You haven't told me what you think about my idea," she said after they cooled down with *piraguas*—shaved ice with flavored syrups. "I can base myself in the UK, at least for a while."

"What I think is that you'll like my estate in Buckinghamshire. It's serene and private." While for all these years it had felt gloomy and isolating, with Luna inhabiting the property it would be as alive as the dancing was in this plaza. He'd never believed that he'd fling open his doors again. The entry to his home. And to his heart. But now he couldn't wait.

He added, "And, if you're not comfortable there, we'll get a place in London."

"I've never been in a real relationship."

"I know. We'll figure it out."

"I don't even know if I want to be in show business anymore."

"We'll figure that out, too. You and I. We'll be able to face anything as long as we're together."

Their joyous dancing lasted until the wee hours, then they fell asleep on the beach on a blanket in the sand in front of the villa. Charlie slept soundly, waking surprised when slumber had come so easily again with her in his arms.

Over morning coffee, Luna checked her phone and had a message from Paris. She excused herself to return the call inside the villa. He wondered whom she knew in Paris and realized he had much to learn about the woman he planned to spend the rest of his life with.

"Well, well," she said as she returned to the front patio after quite a while. "The universe must be tuned in to our master plan."

"What do you mean?" He gestured for her to sit beside him on a lounger on the sand and have some spicy café con leche.

"That was Bernice Dubois."

"The film director?" One of France's

best-known directors, she had been consistently wowing at film festivals and winning awards lately.

"Yes. She saw my interview with Blick Jenson. She's struggled with an eating disorder herself."

"Interesting."

"She's written a script about a woman whose life is almost ruined by it until she's able to get the proper treatment. She just offered me the role."

Joy swelled in him. "You've said you wanted to start making films that were important to you. What did you tell her?"

"That I had to read the script first, of course. But that I was very interested." As the news set in, she added, "Oh, my gosh. Do you know what this could mean for me?"

"I'm so happy for you."

"She asked if I thought my schedule would allow me to spend some time in Paris once I finish the shoot I'm on."

"I love Paris. Which, by the way, is a very short distance from Buckinghamshire," he said with a wily smile.

"I owe so much of it to you. If it hadn't been for you, I wouldn't have had the courage to open up in that interview. You've become a new mirror to see myself in."

"I could say the same about you." He leaned over and cupped her velvety cheek with his hand, brought his lips to hers, both of them giddy with anticipation about the future. "You pulled me out of the darkness. I never expected to shine in the light again. You made my life worth living again. You are simply magical, my love."

"No one has ever loved me just for me. I don't have to prove myself to you. You have no idea how much you've changed my whole being in the blink of an eye. You've given me myself back."

"And I always will, my Luna, my beloved."

They held hands and looked outward, watching the morning sparkle over the Caribbean.

"I'm going to miss Puerto Rico," she said wistfully.

"We'll come back," he said as he went down on one knee in the sand and pulled a small velvet box from his pocket, opening it to reveal a sun-glinted diamond ring. "On our honeymoon. Will you marry me?"

Luna's smile told him everything he needed to know. "I will, Charlie. I will."

EPILOGUE

FRIENDS AND WORK colleagues congregated in the garden until they were told to take their seats because the ceremony was to begin. Luna's family and her Hollywood team were there. Anush was a lovely maid of honor in her pewter-colored dress. And Charlie's COO, Tom, made a dignified best man in his grey suit. Bernice Dubois and Luna's new French friends were in attendance, as well. In the back row, Madison Morgan of the M Dating Agency looked on, the results of her handiwork earning her a well-deserved smile of pride.

Charlie waited at the altar as he watched his future father-in-law walk his magnificent bride down the aisle. She approached in her slinky champagne-colored dress holding a bouquet of flowers she'd requested be picked from this very garden—from the monument that Charlie had planted in his mourning so many years ago.

The memorial garden had become a happy place, where Charlie and Luna came to walk and talk frequently. So much had happened in the months since Luna accepted the acting role with Bernice. The two women had already formed a production company to make films about women's issues and several projects were underway, with others planned. Luna was easily able to base herself in Buckinghamshire. In fact, she had nothing short of a corporate office set up in an unused wing of the mansion. Charlie was delighted that those floors were being used for something important.

As the officiant pronounced them husband and wife, Charlie could not have been more in love with the woman who was now his wife. Their kiss was met with cheers and applause. They had the good wishes of everyone in attendance, most of them knowing what challenging paths Charlie and Luna had had to follow in order to get to this moment.

The sun was out, the flowers were vibrant and the bees were buzzing. Looking up to the light blue sky, he could hardly believe what he saw. A rainbow-striped kite soared up toward the clouds. Where on earth could it have come from? A neighboring property, perhaps? A child at a party having accidentally let go of the line?

A strong feeling of warmth filled Charlie on the inside. He knew what the kite meant. *Thank you, Amelia*, he mouthed.

At the luncheon following the ceremony Charlie and Luna made the rounds, visiting guests at every table. One of his employees asked, "Where are you going on your honeymoon?"

The bride and groom beamed enormous smiles to each other, then answered in unison, "Puerto Rico, of course."

* * * * *

If you missed the previous stories in the Billion-Dollar Matches quartet, then check out

The Princess and the Rebel Billionaire
by Sophie Pembroke
Surprise Reunion with His Cinderella
by Rachael Stewart

And look out for the next book
Indonesian Date with the Single Dad
by Jessica Gilmore
Available next month!

And if you enjoyed this story, check out these other great reads from Andrea Bolter

Wedding Date with the Billionare
Captivated by Her Parisian Billionaire

Available now!